SECRETS OF PHARAOH

PALACE OF THE ORNAMENTS
BOOK FIVE

KYLIE QUILLINAN

First published in Australia in 2024.

ABN 34 112 708 734

kyliequillinan.com

Copyright © 2024 Kylie Quillinan

All rights reserved.

Apart from any use as permitted under the *Copyright Act 1968*, no part may be reproduced, copied, scanned, stored in a retrieval system, recorded, or transmitted, in any form or by any means, without the prior written permission of the publisher. Enquiries should be addressed to Kylie Quillinan at kylie@ kyliequillinan.com.

A catalogue record for this book is available from the National Library of Australia.

Ebook ISBN: 9781922852366

Paperback ISBN: 9781922852373

Large print ISBN: 9781922852380

Hardback ISBN: 9781922852397

Audiobook ISBN: 9781922852472

This is a work of fiction. Any similarity between the characters and situations within its pages and places or persons, living or dead, is unintentional and coincidental.

Cover art by 100 Covers

Edited by MS Novak.

Proudly independent. Please support indie authors by legally purchasing their work.

This work uses Australian spelling and grammar.

LP02112024

CHAPTER 1

"My lady, are you ready?"

Sehener's quiet question brought me back to my surroundings. I had stopped just before the Palace's front doors, with my hand pressed to my belly. *I will protect you,* I promised my unborn son. *He will never harm you. No matter what I have to do, no matter the cost for me, I will keep you safe. And that starts with revealing Pharaoh's crimes.*

"Your transport is probably waiting," Sehener continued.

My transport to Pharaoh's palace where I was to play *senet* with him.

Show Pharaoh what the women of Babylon are made of. My mother's words were as clear as the day she said them to me.

"I'm ready," I said and walked on.

Sehener and Ettu followed me. At the front doors, the day guards, Khaemope and Karpusa, had been replaced with the night guards. One nodded a greeting while the other held the door open for me. I followed the torch-lit path to the gates. They were no more than a looming shadow in the encroaching darkness, slightly ajar in preparation for my arrival. The guards would have been told to expect me.

I stopped so my maids could make any final adjustments they thought necessary. I wore a silvery gown which flowed over my curves and the blue sapphire from Pharaoh was heavy at my throat. I didn't want to wear it, but there was no choice. He was incensed I wore my favourite heart-shaped gem last time. He tore it from my throat and flung it to the floor. I couldn't afford to infuriate him like that again. From now on, I would be the perfect Ornament in his presence. In appearance, at least.

Merytre twitched my skirt one last time to straighten it and Sehener adjusted my wig. They seemed to share a look, and Merytre glanced towards the gates, as if wondering whether the guards would hear us.

"I wish you were permitted to take at least one maid with you," she said.

I only nodded, knowing we couldn't risk saying more where the guards might hear. Meeting with Pharaoh here at the Palace of the Ornaments might be no less safe, but at least my maids could come. When I travelled to his palace, they weren't permitted to accompany me.

"Be safe," Sehener murmured. "One of us will be waiting up for your return."

There was no point in saying I wouldn't be back late. We all knew I had no control over when I returned. I would have to stay until Pharaoh tired of me. Anxiety twisted my belly into knots. Would he expect to lie with me? I had thought myself safe from that until my son was born, but there was no certainty.

"Are you well?" Ettu asked. "You have suddenly gone very pale."

I waved away her question. I could hardly share my thought with the guards standing so close.

"May Isis be with you," Sehener said very quietly.

I gave her a small smile, although it felt so tight, it probably looked more like a grimace.

The palanquin had already arrived. Male slaves lounged

nearby, waiting to carry me to Pharaoh's palace, along with guards who came to escort me. Both slaves and guards were naked to their waists, wearing only the white *shendyt* favoured by the Egyptian men. Their chests and bellies were well muscled, and I averted my eyes before anyone thought I was staring. A portly man, presumably the slave master, was immersed in a loud discussion with the gate guards.

Egyptian men wore much less than those I grew up around and seemed to feel no self-consciousness at having their bodies on display. Khaemmalu's body was just like theirs, his chest smooth and the muscles well defined beneath his linen shirt. My cheeks heated at the thought and I ducked my head, hoping nobody would notice. Thankfully, my wig had braids which dangled to my shoulders and they fell forward to shield my face somewhat.

"Are you ready to leave, my lady?" a guard asked.

"Yes."

He led me to the palanquin and held my hand as I stepped in. It was slightly shocking to have him touch me, given the prohibitions against any male touching one of Pharaoh's Ornaments. I assumed aiding me like this must be an exception, because he didn't try to hide it and nobody reacted, although one slave studied me with what seemed to be a leer. I narrowed my eyes at him and he quickly looked away. The slave master followed my gaze, but apparently saw nothing amiss.

I settled myself on the cushioned bench and smoothed my skirt so it didn't wrinkle. The slave master barked an instruction and the slaves promptly gathered around the palanquin. I clutched the sides as they lifted it onto their shoulders and we set off.

The streets were still busy, presumably folk heading home after work or on their way to do some chore like collecting water. A group of skinny children — three boys and a girl —

watched as we passed. I gave them a little wave and the girl's mouth dropped open.

What would it be like to be a peasant girl, standing in the street as a finely-dressed woman passed in her palanquin? Did she wonder who I was? Did she dare think she had seen a princess, or even a queen, or did she assume I was merely a noble woman?

The possibility she might think me a queen swiftly brought me back to reality. I came to this country thinking I would be queen. A natural assumption given I was sent to marry Pharaoh. It was only later, after my sister arrived, that I learned my father knew all along I wouldn't be queen. He just never told me, and neither did Ishtar.

Immersed in thoughts about what had led me to Egypt, the journey passed quickly. Before I knew it, the slaves lowered the palanquin and a guard stepped forward to help me out. He led me through the palace to a hallway lined with more guards. This was a familiar sight to me by now and clearly signalled my destination.

As I strode past the row of guards, I spotted the one who helped me back to my palanquin after Pharaoh lay with me. I had been distressed and he was kind to me. He gave me an almost imperceptible nod.

The guard at the door ran his hands down my body to check for concealed weapons. Even this was something I had become accustomed to, although no man had ever touched me in such a way before, even Khaemmalu. Or, rather, he hadn't yet. The guard finished his inspection of me, then opened the door and gestured for me to enter.

The chamber was spacious and well appointed, with thick rugs covering the mud brick floor and elegant tapestries on the walls. It wasn't the banquet hall I had dined in with Pharaoh and his queen, Isis, but a smaller, more intimate, chamber. In its centre stood a table with two chairs. A *senet* board was already set out on the table, the playing pieces stacked neatly on each side.

The serving woman wore the usual attire of the women who attended Pharaoh, which was to say, not much at all. Her woven girdle covered nothing other than a thin strip of skin at her waist. I kept my gaze on her face and pretended I didn't see her nakedness. It got easier every time.

"Wine, my lady?" she asked.

"Please."

She brought me a goblet and I wandered around the chamber, looking at the tapestries covering the walls. The first to catch my eye was a lioness who was depicted as almost life-sized. She seemed to look right at me, and although I wasn't particularly good at stitching, I could tell the tapestry was finely made. Her coat looked so real, I was tempted to touch it and see if I could run my fingers through her fur.

"That is Sekhmet, my lady."

I turned to find the serving woman watching me from her station, which was a bench laid out with an assortment of wines and goblets. None of the women who attended Pharaoh had ever spoken to me before other than to offer wine or food, and I was surprised she had volunteered even that much.

"It is very fine work," I said.

"My grandmother stitched it." Her voice was proud.

"Sekhmet is a goddess, as I understand," I said. "Did your grandmother worship her?"

"Yes, she had a very strong affinity with Sekhmet."

"Isn't she supposed to be..." My voice trailed away as I realised that calling the goddess her grandmother had worshipped savage or violent might be offensive. All I knew of Sekhmet was the tale about how she drank a river of blood.

"I can see how she might be misunderstood from a foreigner's perspective," the woman said. "We call her The One Before Whom Evil Trembles. She is a fierce protector of those she loves."

"I know little about her," I admitted.

"You are drawn to her, though, aren't you?" the woman asked.

Surprised, I shot her a look back over my shoulder. Of course, she wouldn't suspect I saw lions everywhere at the moment.

"Yes," I said. "How did you know?"

"Perhaps she has a message for you," she said. "If you feel Sekhmet seeks you, you should pay attention."

Before I could reply, the door opened and two guards swept through. Their presence signalled Pharaoh's imminent arrival, which meant I would have no further opportunity to question the serving woman. She might hold a piece of the puzzle I was trying to put together, but I would probably never see her again.

CHAPTER 2

The guards finished their inspection, then Pharaoh entered. Each time I saw him, I looked for some sign of his crimes. A shadow of guilt on his face, or a nervousness about him. But, of course, Pharaoh was above the law. He wouldn't see his actions as crimes.

He wore the usual *shendyt*, with a blue linen shirt that did little to disguise his enormous belly. His fingers were laden with heavy rings and the wide lapis lazuli collar around his neck looked uncomfortably tight.

He never even glanced at me as he lumbered over to the table with the *senet* board and planted his substantial behind on a chair. The serving woman hurried to offer him wine and I noticed she was careful to stay out of range of grasping hands. Perhaps she had attended him previously. She waited until Pharaoh drained the goblet she handed him and held it up to be refilled. Yes, she had definitely served him before. It was only once he had a full goblet in his hand again that he finally looked at me.

"The Babylonian," he said.

I swallowed my irritated retort, set my wine on the floor, and lay on my belly. Surely he remembered which of his many Ornaments he had invited to play with him? I dined with him not that long ago, me and Hilde. Had he already forgotten my name again?

"Yes, yes," he said.

I got to my feet and gave him a bland smile, trying with everything in me to conceal my hatred.

"Thank you for inviting me, my lord," I said.

He glanced towards the spare chair and I guessed it was intended as an indication that I was to sit. Even as I straightened my skirt over my knees, Pharaoh had already made his first move. He crossed his arms over his chest and leaned back.

I hesitated, considering my options. There were several potential moves I could make, one of which would block his piece.

"Do you not know how to play?" he asked, already irritable, even though it had been my turn for no more than a few moments. Surely he expected I might need time to consider my options.

I moved a playing piece, not the one that would have blocked his.

"Of course, my lord," I said. "I was merely trying to decide."

"Well, don't take so long about it next time." His hand was already on a playing piece.

We traded turns back and forth in silence. I tried not to think about Ishtar. Tried not to imagine his hands around her slender neck. Her body still and limp after he was finished with her. A fierce desire to accuse him of murder rose within me until I had to clamp my mouth shut for fear I would blurt it out. I had no idea what he would do to me if I did, but it definitely wouldn't be pleasant. And there was nobody here who would stand up for me. The serving woman certainly wouldn't, and nor would his own guards. I pushed thoughts of Ishtar away and tried to concentrate on the game.

There came a point where I saw a way I might win. Mindful of Tiye's advice that Pharaoh must always win, I ignored it and moved a different piece. If a novice like myself could spot the error in his game, Pharaoh must be a terrible player. The realisation surprised me. I had thought a living god would be better at his most favoured pastime.

His next move blocked the route I had seen. He grunted and looked pleased with himself, no doubt thinking it was his prowess that prevented my win. He probably couldn't imagine a scenario in which he won by anything other than his own skill.

The urge to speak became overwhelming and I searched for a topic that wouldn't infuriate him. Not my sister. Not Tiye's plan to replace him with her son.

"Have you heard from my father lately?" I asked.

"The Babylon alliance," he muttered absently.

I waited, but he said nothing else.

"My father is Marduk-apla-iddina," I said at last.

"Yes, yes. All is well with the alliance."

"And my father?"

He gave me a quizzical look.

"Is my father well?" I asked. "I have not heard from him for some time."

"I wouldn't know." His tone was rather short now. "We do not discuss such things."

He knew nothing about the health of his best ally? I restrained the huff that wanted to come out of my mouth and searched for a different topic since Pharaoh would make no effort at conversation. But he surprised me.

"I see you wore my gift this time." He sounded snide now, a clear indication he remembered my insult in not wearing it when I dined with him.

So maybe he hadn't forgotten who I was, after all. Perhaps it was a pretence. A reminder I was so far beneath him, I was hardly worth his effort to remember. Did he even recall my sister, or was she already forgotten, just another faceless woman he disposed of once he had tired of her?

"Yes." I searched for an appropriately grateful response. "It was very generous of you."

He huffed and moved one of his pieces.

"I suppose you think your babe might be my heir," he said.

I stared at him blankly for a moment. Why would he say such a thing?

"I know you already have an heir," I said.

He laughed. "Yes, everyone knows, but still every Ornament thinks her child will replace my heir. He won't, you know."

"I didn't expect such a thing."

I could hardly tell him I had entertained the thought, however briefly. I fastened my gaze on the game board and tried not to think about Tiye's plan to put her own son on the throne.

"Even if my son, Ramses, were to go to the West, I have many other sons from many other women," he said. "Women who I favour more than you."

He shot me a disparaging look. My cheeks heated at his blatant acknowledgement of how little I meant to him. Not that I had thought anything else. Who would expect a man with thousands of "wives" to remember any more than a handful of favourites, let alone care for them?

"I wouldn't choose your son even if I had no other sons left alive," he said.

He was deliberately being cruel. There was no other reason he would say that.

"After all," he continued. "You aren't even beautiful. I can hardly nominate an heir from a woman who isn't beautiful. You are not like your sister. It should have been her your father sent to me."

I froze. Surely he didn't say what I thought he did. I must have misheard.

"My lord— " I started, but he cut me off.

"You know you are not as beautiful as her, don't you?" he asked.

I stammered. How could he talk about her like this? Had we been wrong about Ishtar's fate? Did she leave after all? Or had she meant so little to him that he had already forgotten he killed her?

Pharaoh's face turned an interesting shade of red, and I jumped as he swept the pieces from the board, sending them tumbling to the floor.

"Answer when I ask you a question," he yelled. Spittle flew from his mouth, landing on my hand. "I am Pharaoh. I do not repeat myself."

Still, no words came to my lips. All I could do was stare at him.

He let out a roar, then shoved the table. It toppled to the floor with a crash.

He took a step towards me and suddenly my body unfroze. I fled across the chamber. The door was heavy and my hands trembled. I pounded on it.

"Let me out," I cried.

The door opened, only by a couple of hands' widths, but it was enough to push my way through, past the guards who showed no surprise at my panicked departure. I ran down the hallway. If the guards even looked at me as I fled, I never noticed. They did nothing to stop me and that was all that mattered.

At the end of the hallway, I couldn't remember whether to go left or right. I chose at random and kept running.

CHAPTER 3

$\mathcal{I}$ tore along the hallway with no sense of direction. The only thought in my head was to get away. As I ran, I remembered Neferu's strange pendant. An Eye of Horus she called it, and she had gifted me one. I never wore it around my neck as she did, but kept it in my pouch. Filled with a sudden need to hold the amulet, I fumbled for it as I ran.

Behind me, a voice called out.

"My lady!"

My foot slipped out of my sandal, causing me to stumble. I almost fell, but caught myself on the wall at the last moment. The amulet fell from my trembling fingers.

No time to stop. He would catch me if I did.

Abandoning both amulet and sandal, I ran.

Panicked breaths.

Somebody right behind me.

Heart too fast. Can't breathe.

"My lady, wait."

My skirt tangled around my legs. The other sandal slipping off.

A hand grabbed my arm, yanking me to a stop.

I let out a sob. Tried to pull myself from his grasp.

"My lady, please. Stop. I'm not trying to hurt you."

He had me by both arms, holding me firmly. I stopped struggling. There was no point. He was too strong and I couldn't get away. I needed my pendant. Neferu said it would protect me, but it was gone. What would protect me now?

"Stop," he said more firmly. "I am trying to help you."

The haze finally cleared from my gaze and I found myself looking up at the guard who had helped me the first time I visited Pharaoh at his palace.

Of course it wouldn't have been Pharaoh who chased after me. He could barely walk across the chamber without panting, and he would never call me "my lady".

"Can you hear me?" the guard asked.

He still held me by the arms and sudden awareness of the risk, to both him and me, filtered into my mind.

"I hear you," I said. "You should let go."

His hands quickly dropped and he took a step back, although he still watched me with an intensity that suggested he expected me to flee.

It was only now I realised we were in an area of the palace I had never seen before. The hallway here was tiled with a green and blue mosaic, and a pretty pond beneath an open expanse of roof provided a peaceful setting for reflection. When my gaze returned to the guard, he was studying me with a frown.

"What happened in there?" he asked.

"I made him angry," I said. "I thought…"

My voice broke and tears welled. I blinked them away, not wanting to cry in front of him, no matter how kind he seemed.

"You thought what?" His tone was gentle. There was something about him that made me feel like it was all right to tell him. Like I was safe with him.

"I thought he would kill me," I said.

He exhaled, a long breath that wasn't quite a sigh, then shook his head.

"Come," he said. "Let's get you out of here. We will go through a back entrance in case he has guards watching for you at the front. Here."

He held out my sandal and the amulet, but didn't wait for me to put them on. I hurried after him, clutching both items.

"You think he would?" I asked as I caught up.

What had I been thinking? If I hadn't mentioned my father, Pharaoh probably wouldn't have remembered my sister, and I shouldn't have antagonised him by fleeing. I should have stayed and taken whatever punishment he gave me for making him angry. Even if I got out of his palace safely, he had only to send someone to fetch me. They could drag me from my chambers and nobody would raise a finger to stop them. Merytre had heard of women being taken from their chambers. Perhaps this was how it happened. They angered Pharaoh, then fled, and he sent men to bring them back.

"I don't know." He didn't look at me as he spoke, but seemed to be occupied in scanning our surroundings.

He led me through various hallways, past folk who were all occupied with their own business. A few cast curious glances in my direction, but most paid no attention. Perhaps the sight of an unknown woman being escorted through the palace was no uncommon thing. We were alone as we reached a particular door. Still, the guard glanced up and down the hallway before he opened it and ushered me outside.

"You saw nothing," he muttered to the two guards flanking the door.

They both nodded.

"Of course," one said.

"This way, my lady." He set off across a paved expanse. "It is rather a long walk, I'm afraid. We will circle the palace and go to where your palanquin should be."

"Should be?" Already puffing from the effort of keeping up with him, I paused to kick off my other sandal and snatch it from the ground. I could move faster with no shoes than with one.

"It is possible your transport has been dismissed," he said. "There may be guards stationed there to watch for you."

"To take me back to Pharaoh?"

What would he do to me? Have me apprehended? Imprisoned? Or worse?

"You need not be afraid," he said. "I won't let anything happen to you."

"Why are you helping me?"

I studied his profile as we walked. The moon was full tonight, providing enough light to make out his features. A strong chin, a rather prominent nose. Shaved head, like most men here.

"Khaemmalu asked me to watch out for you." He glanced at me briefly, as if to gauge my reaction.

"You are the friend he mentioned." The one who suspected Pharaoh's captain and second disposed of bodies for him.

"Khaemmalu is like my brother. There is nothing I wouldn't do for him."

"He said the same about you."

"He wants you safe," he said. "He asked that I get you out of the palace if you were in any danger. There is a place — a safe place — I am to take you if that happens. He will find you there."

"Is that where we are going now?"

"It depends on whether your transport is where it should be," he said. "If it is, then I think you are safe enough. For now. He usually forgets his anger quickly. You should take care not to cross him again, though. I think you are aware of the risks."

"I am."

We walked in silence for a while. The grounds looked much the same as what I was accustomed to. Paved paths, meticulous flower beds, grassy expanses, and numerous shady trees. Everything perfect, every last blade of grass cut to the exact right height to blend evenly with the others. To see such perfection, nobody would guess the dark secrets this place contained.

"I am sorry about your sister." His voice was stiff now. "I would have helped her if I could, but we were sent away that night."

"Khaemmalu told me. Thank you for helping me tonight. I don't know what I would have done otherwise."

"You seem like a resourceful woman," he said as we rounded the corner of the palace. "I see why Khaemmalu is so enamoured with you."

"He is?" My cheeks were hot and I hoped he couldn't see my blush in the moonlight. "Has he said that?"

"He doesn't need to. I have known him most of my life. The look on his face when he talks about you, I have never seen him like that before."

I was so intent on his words that I wasn't paying attention to where I stepped and caught my toe as we crossed back onto a path. He was quick to grab my arm before I fell. My toe throbbed, but I kept moving. A sore toe was of little consequence right now.

"I don't even know your name," I said.

"Bebi. At your service, my lady."

"You can call me Kassaya. I hardly think we need such formality given the circumstances."

"Lady Kassaya, then. It wouldn't be proper for me to call you anything else."

We said little after that. I was too busy trying to keep up with him to have any breath left for conversation. The palanquin was indeed where it should be, and the slaves lounged nearby on the grass. Their master spotted me approaching and shouted for them to get up. By the time Bebi and I reached them, they were arranged around the palanquin, ready to lift it onto their shoulders and carry me away.

"I think you will be fine from here," Bebi murmured to me. "I will follow a little distance behind you. Don't be afraid. If something happens on the way, I will be there."

"Thank you," I said. "You are a good friend to Khaemmalu."

He gave me a little bow and hurried away. To anyone who had not heard his words, it looked like he headed back to his post. I assumed he would wait somewhere nearby to follow me at an inconspicuous distance.

It was only once I was settled in the palanquin that I realised I should have asked Bebi if he remembered anything else about the night Ishtar disappeared. He could hold the clue to her location without even realising. I no longer had any hope she might be found alive, but I would dearly like to know where her body lay. I had yet to write to my father, and although the news I must send would break his heart, he would surely want to know where she was.

CHAPTER 4

My body was tight with tension as I returned to the Palace, but knowing Bebi followed gave me some reassurance. I didn't let myself look back to see if I could spot him. The slave master might get suspicious and he would probably report anything odd in my behaviour to the administrators. Besides, if Bebi's training was anything like Khaemmalu's, I would never see him unless he wanted me to. But even knowing Bebi watched over me, I still strained to hear any sound of pursuit.

We reached the Palace without incident. The slaves lowered the palanquin and a guard came to help me out. Back within the gates, I meandered along the torch-lit path that led to the Palace, hoping Khaemmalu would be nearby. After such a disastrous evening, I craved the luxury of a little time with him. I was only halfway to the front doors when a bush rustled.

"Come," came his whisper.

I could see nothing within the confines of the shrubbery, but his hand found mine and he led me on. We reached a clearing where a little moonlight made its way between the branches, and there we stood face-to-face, his fingers still holding mine, our bodies no more than a hand's width apart.

"Did something happen?" he asked. "You look upset."

I hesitated, wondering how much to share with him, but Bebi would probably tell him anyway and then Khaemmalu would wonder why I had kept it from him. I already held so many secrets. I didn't want to keep another from the man I loved if it wasn't necessary.

"He asked if I knew I wasn't as beautiful as Ishtar," I said. "When I took too long to answer, he grew angry. He threw the *senet* board on the floor, then tipped over the table. I thought…"

My throat choked and I stopped to compose myself. Khaemmalu's hand tightened around mine, but he said nothing, only waited for me to continue.

"I thought he would kill me," I said at last. "I fled. I got lost, but your friend found me. Bebi. He helped me get back to the palanquin and said he would follow to make sure I got here safely."

"I asked him to watch out for you."

"He told me."

"Are you well?" His voice was husky now.

"Well enough. I was scared. I honestly thought—"

A sob burst out of me. Khaemmalu released my hand and for a moment I mourned the loss of contact, but then he wrapped his arms around me and drew me against his chest. For a few moments, the rest of the world disappeared. All I knew was his arms around me, his body warm against mine, his breath near my ear, steady and unhurried.

"He was wrong to say you aren't as beautiful as your sister," he murmured. "I have always thought you far more beautiful."

Tears came to my eyes, although I couldn't have said whether it was because of his compliment or the mention of Ishtar.

"You don't need to say such a thing," I said against his chest. His thin linen shirt did nothing to stop the heat of his body from reaching me as I breathed in his scent. "I always knew she was more beautiful than me. She was the elegant daughter, the witty one. Everyone knew she would marry an important man. I'm just the younger daughter. Her sister. Nobody special."

"That is far from true," Khaemmalu said. "Your beauty is more striking than hers, and there is a genuineness and a kindness to you that I never saw in her."

I was thankful he couldn't see my tears with my face pressed against his chest. Nobody had ever thought me to be the special one before. He held me for a few moments longer, then his hands slid down my arms to capture my fingers.

"You should go," he said. "The longer we are here, the greater the risk of someone seeing us."

I left reluctantly. The heat of his hands on me lingered as I hurried along the path and through the Palace. At my chambers, I knocked and Ettu let me in. It took her no more than a glance to realise something was wrong.

"What happened?" she asked.

I sank onto a couch, thankful everyone else had already retired to their bedchambers, and tried to find the words to explain. It came out haltingly. Ettu's face showed her horror.

"Thank Marduk Khaemmalu's friend was there," she said.

"I thought you didn't believe in Marduk anymore."

She shot me an aggrieved look and I regretted my comment.

"Maybe…" Ettu's voice trailed away.

I waited, but she said nothing else.

"Go on," I said

She spoke with obvious reluctance. "Maybe you should leave. Ahmose can surely get more of the herb she needs for her special potion, or Khaemmalu might have a way of getting you out of the gates. You could take your jewels. They were given to you, so I think they are yours to do as you want with them, and they are valuable enough that you could go wherever you wish."

"By myself? I can't even imagine doing such a thing."

I would have to leave the country if I fled the Palace. A lengthy sea voyage to a destination which would be just as foreign to me as Egypt originally was. Another new country to adapt to, one in which I didn't even speak the language this time. Ahmose had taught us Egyptian on our journey from Babylon, and although I wasn't very fluent when we arrived, I had grown increasingly comfortable with it in the months since then.

"I would come with you," Ettu said.

But the look on her face said she offered with reluctance. I knew why. If I fled, there would be no time to get a message to Half to come with us. He was somewhere in Pharaoh's palace, searching for confirmation of Ishtar's fate. I couldn't ask Ettu to leave the man she loved.

My purpose in being here was to prevent war between Egypt and Babylon. How could I risk the safety of a whole country for my own sake? My father sent me here for a reason and it seemed all I could do was make the best of the situation.

CHAPTER 5

As my maids bathed and dressed me the next morning, I was so absorbed in my thoughts that I hardly noticed their attentions. Was Pharaoh still angry about last night? Would he send a messenger to summon me? Had anyone seen me with Bebi and would that cause problems for him?

Then there was both Khaemmalu and Ettu's comments that I should leave. But how could I? Even if I pretended the fate of the alliance didn't matter to me, how could I flee alone? Khaemmalu's sister lived here in Thebes and she was his only family. And neither Ettu nor Tall would want to leave without Half, anymore than I would want to leave him behind. I doubted Tall would leave Sehener either, and Merytre was newly married to Sutem. Ahmose was the only one of my closest companions who didn't have anyone to keep her here. She might, perhaps, come with me. But if I fled, would those who stayed behind suffer some retribution from the administrators?

There were also my fledging friendships with other Ornaments to consider. Tiye, for one. She was not an easy woman to get to know, but she had started to show me some of her real self lately. Henutmire, who I often broke my fast with in the dining chamber. She had proven herself to be a compassionate woman, and she was one of the few who didn't try to pretend Ishtar had returned to Babylon as the administrators claimed. Gilukhipa, Ineni and Neferu. I didn't know any of them well, but they had been welcoming to me, and I had thought that, with time, we would become friends. I had never had female friends before and I was reluctant to give up that opportunity.

What would the rest of my maids think if I fled? They held me in high regard, or at least I had been told they did. Mutnofret, Hemetre, Ipu, Khensa, Nebetah, Tuya. Abar was the only exception. I had sought information about her sister for her — and it cost me a treasured hairbrush — but when we found out Atahar had disappeared, Abar blamed me for not acting soon enough. She seemed to think I had far more power than I did.

Ettu's voice broke into my thoughts.

"Where is Abar?" she asked, as if she knew I was thinking about the girl.

"I haven't seen her today," Nebetah said.

"She sleeps in the same dormitory as me," Ipu said. "But I don't think she came to bed last night."

"Has anyone seen her since yesterday morning?" Ettu's tone was sharp now.

Nobody had.

"Is something wrong?" I asked.

Abar had never failed to attend me with the rest of my maids, but she was very distressed yesterday when I told her that her sister was believed to have died. She would be even more upset if she knew I saw Atahar at the House of Life some weeks ago. Even now, the memory of watching the knife descend into the woman's belly made me flinch. I hadn't realised at the time she was Abar's sister, and it wasn't her we were looking for that night.

We never did confirm whether Nebtu's body was there too, although we learned an unidentified woman had been brought in. It might have been Nebtu, or it might not. We would never know now after so much time had passed.

"I am going to see Panouk." Ettu was already on her way to the door. "Merytre, would you look after everything here?"

She was gone before I could ask why it was so urgent that she see the administrator immediately.

My maids were somewhat subdued after that, their usual chatter more sporadic than usual. At last, I was attired to their satisfaction and they filed out, offering good wishes for my day on their way. Merytre returned a discarded gown to my clothing chest, smoothing it carefully so the linen wouldn't wrinkle. They had dressed me in it earlier before deciding I should wear something else, an occurrence that happened with some regularity. Sehener went off to unlock Tall's door and return some jewellery to the chest we kept in there.

Some of my cosmetics jars were out of place, so I stopped to rearrange them. Ettu was meticulous about keeping them tidy and she would be unhappy to see my maids had left them in disorder.

As I moved a perfume bottle back in line with the rest of my cosmetics, an earthy, herbal smell filled the chamber. I froze, my hand still on the bottle. I might have thought one of the perfumes had spilled if I didn't recognise the fragrance and know it was one I had never worn. It was frankincense and it reminded me sharply of Ishtar. She used to favour a more musky scent, but once she came to Egypt, she had worn something that smelled just like this.

But when I turned to see who had entered the chamber, I found myself alone. The scent still lingered, though, so whoever she was, she must have only just left. I hadn't noticed any of my maids wearing such a scent, but obviously one of them must, and she had returned briefly for some reason.

Sehener passed by on her way back to the sitting chamber, but stopped when she saw me.

"My lady?" She gave me a quizzical look. "Are you well? You have the strangest expression."

"Did you see who was just here?" I asked.

"Here? In your bedchamber?" Her face became confused. "Nobody."

"Someone was here. I smelled her perfume."

"I can see your door from Tall's," she said. "Nobody has entered your bedchamber since the others left."

Indeed, the scent had faded and now I wasn't even certain it had been there in the first place.

"Never mind," I said, feeling a little foolish. "I must have been mistaken."

Ettu was gone for some time and when she finally returned, she looked unusually harried.

"Panouk has not seen her," she said. "She is not in her dormitory either. I sent a runner to check with the healers and the kitchen, but I don't know where else to look."

"Do you think we should be concerned?" I asked, seeing how she frowned. "She must be safe enough."

After all, we knew the threat to the women here was from Pharaoh, and Abar had no contact with him. Ettu shrugged.

"It is rather odd," she said. "She might have gone off somewhere wanting to be alone for a while, but given how distressed she was yesterday, I would like to know she is well."

After all, Abar had a sister to grieve for. I knew what that was like.

"I can get Sutem to ask if any of the guards have seen her," Merytre offered.

"I will come with you," Ettu said.

"Tell him we just want to know where she is," I said. "She doesn't need to be sent back if they find her."

Merytre hurried Ettu out the door with remarkable haste. I restrained a smile at how Merytre brightened at the unexpected reason to see Sutem. It felt like an inappropriate time to smile, although I wasn't sure Abar's disappearance needed to be taken quite so seriously. She must be somewhere within the Palace or its grounds, and she would come back when she was ready. There was no way she could have caught Pharaoh's eye. Not from here.

I settled myself on the couch to wait for their return. It was a little cooler today, hopefully an indication the long-overdue turning of the season was finally on its way. Tall and Sehener stood together at the window talking quietly, or more likely, Sehener was doing the talking while Tall listened.

Ahmose was in her usual chair, her feet propped up on a foot-stool. She gave me a meaningful look, then glanced towards the window, as if signalling she had something to say which she didn't want the others to hear. If that was the case, it must be about the bribe for Messui, who worked in Pharaoh's personal library. He was one of only two men who had access to the locked chamber in which the books of magic were kept. I had given Ahmose Ishtar's gift from Pharaoh — a red gem the size of a hen's egg — to offer Messui in exchange for access to spells of power.

"I received something from our friend last night." Ahmose's voice was low.

"Oh?" I kept my tone casual and tried to pretend I wasn't all that interested.

Neither Tall nor Sehener were paying attention to us right now, and Ahmose spoke quietly enough that they probably couldn't make out her words, but I didn't want to spark their interest. Tall, in particular, might come sit with us if he thought we discussed something exciting. Marduk knew he had little enough to pass his day with. I could only hope Sehener continued to keep him occupied over at the window.

"Unfortunately it was not what we were looking for," Ahmose said. "I will return it and ask for another."

I tried not to sigh. It was unrealistic to think the first scroll

Messui sent might have contained a powerful spell, and I hadn't realised until that moment how much I had hoped for it. A fast solution to the problem of a man who thought himself to be a god.

"You will need patience," Ahmose said, as if she knew what I was thinking. "What you desire will not come easily."

My plan was still somewhat unclear in my mind, but I intended to find a way to expose Pharaoh's crimes. Tiye also had a plan, although hers involved removing Pharaoh in order to put her own son in his place. She had invited me to work with her, but the knowledge that Tiye — and Tiye alone — had chosen the man she thought best suited to be the next ruler, made me uneasy. That, surely, was a greater decision than any one mortal should make.

Perhaps, in time, our separate plans would create change for Egypt, but for now, I would keep my plan to myself. Nobody other than me, Ahmose, and her mystery contact knew what I sought from Pharaoh's library.

CHAPTER 6

Merytre and Sehener returned with confirmation Sutem would alert the other guards to our search for Abar. He would send a runner to my chambers if anyone saw her.

"I suppose that is all we can do," I said.

The administrators would hardly be interested in the problem of a missing servant.

Ettu stood in front of her usual couch, but made no move to sit.

"What is it?" I asked, noticing her frown.

"I don't suppose..." she started, then shook her head. "No, she wouldn't."

"You think she might have gone to find her sister?" Sehener asked. "I wondered that too."

"She can't have," I said. "How would she get out through the gates?"

Ettu shrugged and finally sat down. "I'm not sure anybody would try to stop her, but regardless, she is a determined woman. I think if she wanted to get out, she would find a way."

"Then why did she stay so long?" I asked. "She made it clear she hated being here."

"She didn't know where her sister was," Ettu pointed out. "She wouldn't leave if there was the possibility Atahar was here within the Palace. After all, if one sister is assigned here, it would be reasonable to assume the other is, too."

"But we know… She knows…" I couldn't make myself say it.

"She doesn't believe Atahar is really dead." Ettu's tone was gentler now. "You know what that is like. It isn't something a person can believe easily."

"I smelled her perfume earlier." The words tumbled out without thought. I didn't need to clarify I meant Ishtar, not Atahar. Ettu would understand.

"In your bedchamber?" Sehener asked. "Is that why you asked me who had been there?"

"It is nothing," I said.

Merytre and Sehener exchanged glances.

"You have been under an enormous amount of pressure lately," Ettu said. "It would be no surprise if…"

"If?" I tried to imitate the raised eyebrows look Tiye often gave me.

Ettu's mouth twitched and I figured I must look more comical than intimidating.

"It would be no surprise if you started imagining things," she said. "Things that gave you a reason to pretend Lady Ishtar is still here with us."

I only shook my head, not wanting to argue with her. I didn't imagine it. I had smelled Ishtar's perfume. I might not know why or how, but I knew it was real.

Several hours passed before a runner boy came with a message from Sutem. We made him wait while Sehener locked Tall away in his bedchamber, and by the time Merytre opened the door, the boy was hopping from foot to foot. He stopped and stood up straight, pulling his shoulders back as he prepared to deliver his message.

"Sutem says he has found what his wife is looking for," the boy said. He was a skinny thing, no more than perhaps nine or ten years, but he spoke clearly, and it was obvious he took his job seriously. "He says if she will go to him when she can, he will return it to her."

Merytre thanked him and closed the door. She gave me a questioning look.

"You had better go then," I said. "Before she disappears again. Take Ettu and Sehener with you."

Not that I thought there was much point sending all three women. If Abar didn't want to come with them, what could they do? They could hardly carry her back kicking and screaming.

Sehener passed me the key to Tall's door, then the three women left. Ahmose moved to get up, but I waved at her to stay.

"Sit," I said. "I can bar the door. I need to let Tall out anyway. But before I do, is there anything else you can tell me about the scroll you received?"

"It contained no more than minor magics," she said. "Mostly such as a farmer might want. A spell to make a herd more productive. One to heal a sickening swine. Another to locate a lost animal. Nothing that would be of use to us."

"Can I see it?"

"I returned it to my contact early this morning." She gave me a steady look. "Regardless, I didn't realise you could read Egyptian."

"I can't."

It was a daft request. What good was seeing the scroll if I couldn't understand it? But I wanted to see it. To touch it. To know I held power in my hands, even if it wasn't the kind of power that would make Pharaoh tremble before me. How did Tiye intend to remove him? Perhaps she, too, sought spells of power.

"I will show you the next one." Ahmose must have wondered why I wanted to see it, but she didn't ask.

"So what happens now?"

"My contact will return the scroll to Messui when she can, and hopefully by then he will have another for us to look at."

"And we keep doing that over and over."

"Yes." She gave me a steady look. "We keep doing that until we find what you are looking for."

CHAPTER 7

*E*ttu, Merytre and Sehener returned with a sullen-faced Abar trailing behind them.

"Abar, come sit down," I said as the girl stood in the doorway. She seemed hesitant to follow the women into my chambers, even though she was here almost every morning. "I am pleased you are well."

"You think I am well?" She gave me a fierce glare.

I stammered as I tried to find a reply, but Ettu saved me.

"My lady was concerned for your wellbeing," she said to Abar. "She merely wanted to know you were safe."

"Yet she shows no concern for my sister," Abar shot back. "She knows my sister is missing and she does nothing to find her."

"Abar, I'm sorry." Ettu set her hand on the girl's shoulder, but Abar shrugged her off. "We have as much information as we are likely to get. If anything more is learnt of your sister's fate, you can be assured we will tell you."

"It is not enough." Abar shared her glare between Ettu and me. "She knows what it is like to have a sister disappear. She should try harder."

I hated that I knew more about Atahar's fate than Abar did, but I couldn't risk telling her. She was too unpredictable. Marduk only knew what she might do with that information. She would certainly try to find out more, maybe to prove me wrong, and that might mean she would tell someone what she knew. And when they asked how she knew, she would reveal the information came from me, and the administrators would demand to know how I had seen such a thing.

"Perhaps my lady could send a messenger to the House of Life?" Merytre suggested. "With a description of Abar's sister?"

"That is a fabulous idea," Ettu said quickly. "My lady, I can go find a runner boy immediately. Abar could come with me to describe her sister to him. We can ask whether any unidentified women matching Atahar's description have been brought in during the last couple of months."

It was a sensible suggestion and I wished someone had thought of it sooner. Perhaps if I had offered to send a messenger to the House of Life, Abar would not be so angry with me. It was odd, this desire I had to placate her, but there was something about her that made me long to do just that. When she glared at me the way she did, I found it hard to remember it was I who was the mistress and she the servant.

"Please do," I said to Ettu. "And tell the runner I want a response as soon as possible."

"Come on, then." Ettu gave Abar a little push towards the door. "Let's go find a runner."

"I am coming back here after that," Abar said fiercely. "I will sit here in these chambers and wait for his return."

I understood why she wanted to, but it would mean Tall had to stay locked in his bedchamber for however many hours it took the runner to go to the House of Life and return. Ettu responded before I could think of what to say.

"You look very tired." She ushered Abar out with her hand on the girl's back. "You should go to your dormitory and rest. I will tell Panouk you must be excused from kitchen duties today and I will personally fetch you the moment the runner returns."

The door closed behind them before Abar could respond. Merytre slid the bar into place and Sehener hurried off to let Tall out.

"I think that is the most you can do for her," Sehener said as she settled into her usual spot beside Tall. She sat close enough to him that their legs must have been touching, but Tall didn't move away. His hands on his thighs were tight balls, as if he tried to stop himself from flapping them.

"And it is far more than most Ornaments would," Merytre added.

She, too, came to sit down, her hands immediately busy with the needlework she had left on her chair. She was still working on the narcissus design she hoped I would hang in my bedchamber. I would have to, of course. I could hardly refuse after she had spent so many hours stitching it for me, but I felt rather odd about the prospect, as if the flowers were reminding me I had yet to remember what they said to me. There was a message in the recurring dreams. I just had to figure out what it was, and how the narcissus were connected to the lions.

At last, a knock came. My heart pounded, even though I knew it would surely be Ettu.

"It is just me," came her voice. "I am alone."

Even so, Tall slipped away to his bedchamber while Merytre let Ettu in.

"You found a runner?" My question was pointless. Ettu would not have returned, and without Abar, if she hadn't.

"Yes, and he understands the matter is urgent. He will report to you as soon as he returns."

"And Abar?" I asked.

"She wanted to come back and wait. I dissuaded her for obvious reasons." Tall returned as she was speaking and she acknowledged him with a nod. "She wasn't happy about it, but I convinced her to go rest for a while. I expect she will return soon, though."

"Go!" Tall said.

"Not yet," I said. "The runner won't be back for at least a few hours. You can't spend all day locked away."

"Sad! Worried!"

I hesitated, but Sehener understood before I untangled who he meant.

"You are right," she said to him. "Abar is concerned for her sister. But she isn't here right now. There is no need for you to rush back to your bedchamber."

Tall gave her a bashful smile. He still seemed surprised at how easily Sehener understood him.

"Did Sutem say where he found her?" I asked.

"Hiding near the gates," Merytre said. "Sutem thought she was waiting for a chance to slip out."

She had probably intended to go to Pharaoh's palace and search for her sister. Guilt washed over me at the reminder that I held the definitive proof of Atahar's fate that Abar needed.

"We will send for Abar when there is news for her," I said.

I dreaded that conversation. Even if the priests from the House of Life confirmed they had prepared Atahar's body, Abar wouldn't welcome the news because it would still mean her sister was truly dead. If only she understood how intimately I comprehended her pain.

CHAPTER 8

Several hours passed before the runner knocked. Even though I knew it surely must be him, my heart beat a little faster at the possibility it might be a summons from Pharaoh calling me to account for making him so angry and then running away.

Tall slipped away to his bedchamber, and Sehener with him, while Ettu waited to open the door. The runner was a lanky boy of about eight years, young enough that his mostly-shaved head still bore the odd sidelock children here wore. He bobbed a quick bow.

"My lady, the chief embalming priest confirms a woman matching the description you gave was taken to the House of Life some weeks ago." His voice was calm and clear, and he spoke with a gravity that was unusual for such a young child. "She received appropriate treatments and blessings, but as her name was unknown, she was consigned to a tomb for the poor."

It was only as he delivered his message that I realised I should have sent Ishtar's description as well. Maybe she, too, had been prepared at the House of Life. She might still be there. After all, Ahmose said the full embalming process took up to seventy days.

Why hadn't we thought to ask? I supposed I hadn't expected her to be treated with that much respect.

I opened my mouth, but stopped as Ettu cleared her throat. She shot me a warning look, as if she knew exactly what I was about to say.

"I assume the priest knows the location of the tomb?" she asked the boy.

He gave her a startled look.

"I am afraid I didn't ask," he said. "You didn't tell me you wanted to know such a thing."

"Go back and ask," she said. "Tell the priest her sister wants to see the body."

I expected him to complain since it was quite a walk to the House of Life, and he'd already been there and back once today, but he only bowed and trotted away. Ettu closed the door and slipped the bar into place.

"If he returns with confirmation of the tomb's location, will Abar need Panouk's permission to leave the grounds?" She gave Merytre a questioning look.

"Servants are permitted to come and go," Merytre said. "The gate guards have given me no problems since I moved in with Sutem. I'm not sure about Abar, though. Since she was brought as a war prisoner, I don't think she will be allowed to leave at will, and even if Panouk gives permission, she will need an escort. I'm sure Sutem would be happy to take her."

"So the night we went to the House of Life, it was only Tall and I who needed Ahmose's potion?" I asked. "You and Ettu could have just walked through the gates and nobody would have stopped you?"

"I suppose so." The look on Merytre's face said she hadn't considered that.

I hated to think we might have wasted the precious special ingredient Ahmose used in her invisibility potion.

"Where is Ahmose?" Ettu asked, seeming to know, as she so often did, exactly what I was thinking about.

Merytre shrugged and took up her stitching again. It was Sehener who answered from her perch beside Tall.

"She said something about needing to speak with someone," she said. "She only mumbled it as she left, though, so perhaps I didn't hear her properly."

Maybe she had gone to see her contact again, the mystery woman — or, at least, I assumed she was a woman — facilitating her messages to the librarian, Messui. If Sehener wondered about Ahmose's errand, she didn't ask.

While we waited for the runner's return, I stretched out on the couch and dozed. I had slept restlessly again last night, which seemed to be a far too common occurrence. Half-remembered dreams about lions and flowers and men dragging me from my bedchamber lingered.

The women chatted quietly while they stitched. Tall said nothing, as usual, and when I checked what he was doing, he had stretched out with his feet on a footstool, seemingly asleep.

The runner finally came with word that the tomb in which the woman believed to be Atahar had been interred was already sealed. It wouldn't be possible for Abar to see her, not that I imagined she would get what she wanted from the experience anyway.

From what I understood, Atahar's body would be preserved in natron salt and then wrapped in many layers of linen. I couldn't imagine how anyone would recognise a loved one like that. It was rather strange to me, this Egyptian belief about the continuing importance of the earthly body even after death.

The boy waited, shifting slightly from foot to foot, as if he expected to be sent back to the House of Life for a third time, and I didn't miss the relief that crossed his face when I dismissed him.

"Abar will be so disappointed," Sehener said after the boy left.

Ettu nodded her agreement. "I suppose there is no way now we can be sure it was definitely her sister."

Again, I saw the woman in my mind's eye. Her dark limbs, her long fingers. How long would it be before I stopped seeing her image imprinted on my mind?

"I am certain she must be Abar's sister," I said.

"There certainly was a resemblance," Ettu said. "But I have heard many Kushites were captured at the same time. It could be just another woman from their homeland."

I didn't miss that she used the same word as Abar did for herself, rather than the derogatory term of Nubian as the Egyptians did.

"It could be," I conceded. "But a woman disappeared and there is a body matching her description. Wouldn't it seem likely those two things are related?"

Ettu shrugged. "It does. I am merely pointing out we assume a connection we cannot prove."

"Do you think that will be enough for Abar?" Sehener asked. "She was terribly upset earlier."

"It will have to be, won't it?" Ettu said. "If the tomb is sealed, this is as much as we can give her."

"I can't imagine it would be pleasant for her to see her sister's body in a tomb of poor and unknown folk anyway," Merytre added.

I left them to their speculation and made no further comment. I had a feeling it didn't matter whether this was as much as I could give Abar or not. It wouldn't be enough for her and I couldn't blame her for that.

Merytre and Sehener went off to find Abar. I passed the time waiting by silently rehearsing what I would say to her. But when they returned, the hopeful look on the girl's face made my carefully practiced speech fly right out of my head. Obviously neither Merytre nor Sehener had prepared her for the news.

"The body of a woman matching your sister's description was taken to the House of Life several weeks ago," I said.

Abar's face changed, the expectant look replaced with her usual surly one.

"Can you be sure it is Atahar?" she asked.

"We can't be completely certain, but it seems likely."

She gave me a frosty glare.

"Seems likely?" she repeated. "Do you think that is good enough?"

"Abar," Ettu said, although her voice wasn't quite as stern as it usually was when she corrected the girl. "My lady has made every attempt to get information for you."

Abar gave no indication she heard Ettu, but focussed all her attention on me. Her glare was like a fire burning right through me.

"I want to see her," she said. "I want to see her body."

"I'm afraid that won't be possible," I said.

She narrowed her eyes at me and I clamped my lips together, trying to resist the urge to placate her.

"You are a wife of Pharaoh," she said. "You can make it possible."

"She has already been interred and the tomb is sealed."

"Then get it unsealed."

"I can't," I said. "I don't have that kind of power."

"Then tell Pharaoh to do it for me." Abar crossed her arms over her chest and glared at me.

"Abar." Ettu's voice was firmer this time. "Remember your place."

"My place," Abar shot Ettu a hostile look, "is at home with my sister. *This* is not my place."

"I'm sorry," I said. "I know the uncertainty is hard."

"Yes." Abar's glare returned to me in full force. "You know and yet you still refuse to help."

"There is really nothing else I can do." My words sounded weak, even to me, despite their truth. "I wish I could do more."

"You wish," she scoffed. "All I hear from you is no and can't and wish. You speak, but you do nothing. I will not do nothing."

She whirled around and was gone before I could say anything else.

Ettu closed the door behind her.

"Well," was all she said.

CHAPTER 9

Babar's accusation that I did nothing but talk felt painfully accurate. Even after I went to bed that night, her words haunted me. *All I hear is no and can't and wish. You speak but you do nothing.* I didn't want that to be the case, but I truly didn't have the power she thought I did. Or did I? There were two people I knew who might be able to help her — Tiye and Khaemmalu — and I knew which was more likely to be amenable.

I rose from my bed and dressed in the first gown I pulled from a clothing chest. Setting a wig over my bald scalp, I hoped it was reasonably straight. The soft glow of lamplight from the sitting chamber told me someone was still up. Ettu, most likely. But to my surprise, it was Ahmose.

She sat in her favourite chair with one hand pressed to her chest.

"Ahmose? Are you well?"

She seemed startled to see me.

"Yes, Princess, don't worry about me," she said.

"What is the matter?" I took in her ashen appearance and the way she seemed to breathe too heavily. "Are you ill?"

"No, no." She let her hand drop to her lap. "Just feeling a little uncomfortable tonight. My chest is tight. But I assume you didn't get out of bed just to check on an old woman."

She would have already guessed I intended to go out. If I was merely coming to get a drink or to sit up for a while, I wouldn't have bothered to dress myself.

"I can't sleep," I said. "I'm going for a walk. Do you want to accompany me?"

I expected she would agree since we still tried to ensure nobody went out alone, but to my surprise, she grimaced.

"I think it would be too much for me right now," she said. "I will bar the door behind you, though, and wait for your return."

"Should I fetch a healer?" I asked.

"No, no." She leaned back and closed her eyes. "I am sure I will feel better in a while. I just need to sit. You go. I will bar the door behind you."

I hesitated, wondering if I should stay, but she didn't open her eyes again and seemed to breathe more normally now.

"Wake Ettu or Sehener if you feel worse," I said. "Send them to fetch a healer."

She gestured for me to go, although she didn't open her eyes. Out in the hallway, I waited, but didn't hear Ahmose come to bar the door. Maybe she had fallen asleep. I didn't want to go back in and disturb her if that was the case. Perhaps she hadn't been sleeping well lately either. Marduk knew the hot nights were oppressive. Even if the door wasn't barred, the noise of someone trying to enter my chambers would surely wake her.

As I turned a corner, I collided with someone and found myself uncomfortably close to Amankhau. We both quickly moved away. I could still feel his hands on my arms, and I longed to go back to my chambers and wash my skin.

"My lady." He gave me a bow that was brief enough to be insulting.

"Administrator."

I moved to walk around him, but he stopped me with an upraised hand.

"I heard you inspected Lady Ishtar's chambers," he said. "I trust you found everything in order."

I gave him a frosty glare.

"If everything was in order, my sister would have been in them," I said.

"I merely meant—" He stopped to clear his throat and seemed unusually uneasy. "I trust you found her belongings as they should be."

"Something I noticed is that she didn't appear to have taken anything with her," I said. "Surely a woman who was planning to ask to go home, would take at least a few favourite things as she left."

"Yes, well." He cleared his throat again. "Should I assume you will make arrangements for her belongings?"

"Arrangements?"

"To remove them," he said. "The chambers will be reassigned in due course. I can send servants to pack up her things if you would prefer."

"You will do no such thing." I gave him my best imitation of Tiye's haughty glare. "When my sister returns, she will expect everything to be as she left it."

After all, I couldn't afford for him to question how I knew she definitely wouldn't be coming back. As far as Amankhau was concerned, I knew only as much as the administrators had told me, which was that Ishtar had asked to be sent home. Given the suddenness of her departure, it wasn't unreasonable for me to hope she might change her mind.

Amankhau shifted his weight from foot to foot. I'd never seen him look so uncomfortable. He was normally smooth — too smooth really — and gave the impression that everything occurred exactly as he intended.

"As you are aware—" he started, but I cut him off.

"I think I am probably aware of much more than you expect," I said. "Now, if you will excuse me."

I strode away before he could respond.

I shouldn't have said that. I didn't need Ettu here to tell me it was a mistake. We were all but certain Amankhau was complicit with the women who disappeared, although we didn't know the depth of his involvement. I might have just made a target of myself. Again.

CHAPTER 10

I didn't look back to see Amankhau's reaction, but walked swiftly, trying to give the impression I had somewhere to be without appearing to flee. At the front doors, the night guards gave me polite nods.

I chose a path that meandered through the shrubbery, hoping the multitude of sheltered spots would allow Khaemmalu to reveal himself. I only sought him to see if he could do anything for Abar, or at least that was what I told myself. I tried not to think about how much I wanted him to touch me again, even if it was just a brush of his fingers against mine. How desperately I longed for his kiss.

If he would kiss me once more, that would be enough. I would make the memory last through the rest of my life. There was no possibility of anything else between us. He was a guard and I was one of the women he was both sworn to protect and forbidden to touch. With rumours of Hydna's affair with the butler, Weren, still swirling, folk would surely be watching for signs of anyone else entertaining illicit liaisons.

I walked for some time with no sign of Khaemmalu. Disappointment welled within me, but I tried to pretend I hadn't really expected to see him tonight. After all, the Palace grounds were vast and he couldn't always patrol just this one area between the front doors and the gates.

It was only as I finally turned back that the bushes rustled. I stopped, my heart pounding, although I couldn't have said whether it was from anticipation or fear. There were no lions in the grounds, I reminded myself. The lions were only in my dreams.

"Khaemmalu?" I whispered.

"Back here," came his soft reply.

I left the path without hesitation and followed his voice into the shadows. The darkness was absolute and I could see nothing. My sandal caught on something, but Khaemmalu's arms were around me before I could fall, other than against his chest.

His heat burned through the thin linen of my gown. I should pull away, peel myself from his body, but I couldn't move. His hands, which had grasped my arms as I fell, slid down to my waist, and he seemed no more inclined to move away than I was.

"Hello," he said softly, his voice near my ear.

"Hello." I breathed the word into his chest. My hands had found their way to his shoulders, although I had no memory of doing such a thing, or even of deciding to do it.

"I hoped to see you tonight," he said.

"You did?"

I pulled away from his chest and tried to make out his face. My eyes had adjusted somewhat to the darkness, but I could still see nothing of his features. His long nose, the strong jaw. I knew them by memory, even if not by touch.

"Of course," he said. "And you hoped to see me."

"You assume. Maybe I merely wanted a walk."

He chuckled softly and his hands slid up my ribs. My breath was shaky. His touch was intimate and for a moment I couldn't even remember what we were talking about.

"You wouldn't have left the path otherwise." His fingers trailed back down to my waist, leaving heat in their wake.

My breath hitched, and for a moment, I couldn't remember how to speak.

"Maybe I thought you had something important to tell me," I said.

"Let's be honest with each other, Kassaya." His fingers trailed around to my back, leaving ribbons of tingling skin. "Whatever this is, however much we have to hide it, we can at least be honest with each other."

I swallowed, hard, and finally found my voice. Sheltered by the darkness and safe in his arms, I could be brave.

"I left the path because I wanted to see you," I said.

His mouth found mine and he lingered there, kissing me until my breath was rough and my mind empty of any thoughts other than about his lips on mine, his body pressed against me, and the way his hands were doing things I'd never even imagined.

When he finally pulled away and took a step back, I longed to follow his mouth, to capture his lips with my own, but I didn't have the courage to do such a thing. Instead I smoothed my wig and tried to give the appearance of someone who is regularly kissed in such a way. Thank Marduk for the darkness. I might just get away with it since he couldn't see my flushed cheeks.

"Kassaya, you..." His voice trailed away and I waited, still breathless, for him to continue. "I have never felt like this before. There is something about you that makes me forget everything else."

"I know," I whispered. "I feel it too."

His hand found mine, his fingers interlinking through my own. My body knew how to respond to him, even though no man had ever held my hand like this before.

"We have to be careful," he said. "So very careful. I couldn't bear it—" His voice choked and he was silent for a few moments. "I couldn't bear it if we were caught and you were..."

"I know the punishment is severe."

"Fire, for you," he said. "Or thrown to the crocodiles. Impalement for me."

I caught my breath. I had known the punishment for an affair, but somehow hadn't considered its application to myself. I would not be an exception. If we were caught, we would both be executed. If I hadn't met Khaemmalu, I wouldn't be able to comprehend why Hydna risked what she did to be with Weren. But I did understand. Marduk save me, but I did.

We were silent for a few moments and, briefly, he let go of my hand. Was it worth the risk? Was anything worth such a risk? But I only had to feel the touch of his hand against mine, his breath by my ear, to know I would risk everything for a few more moments with him.

I could be sensible. End this affair here and now. Spend the rest of my life trying to pretend I didn't love Khaemmalu. That I didn't want him with everything in me. But it would be a lie. A life half-lived. And now I'd had a taste of him, I couldn't bear to think of giving him up.

"I'm willing to take the risk if you are," I said.

His fingers left my hands. He grabbed my hips and pulled me against him.

"There is nothing I want more," he said just before his mouth claimed mine again.

CHAPTER 11

It was quite some time before either Khaemmalu or I spoke again. He sat with his back against a tree trunk and I leaned against his chest. The leaf litter beneath us was cool and slightly damp.

Khaemmalu's fingers trailed up and down my arm, leaving pimples in their wake. His hand wandered to my belly and thoughts of my babe suddenly broke through my haze. Khaemmalu still didn't know I carried Pharaoh's child.

My belly was only slightly rounded, certainly not enough to reveal the babe's existence. I had to tell him, though. Only a handful of folk knew, but as my belly grew, so would the talk. I didn't want such speculation to reach Khaemmalu before I told him myself.

"I heard your maid's sister went to the West," he said.

I didn't bother asking how he heard. The guards seemed to know everything. Maybe the runner boys shared their news, or perhaps Sutem told him about finding Abar hidden in the grounds. Maybe Khaemmalu knew about Atahar before I did, but didn't realise I would want to know.

"My maid wants to view the body," I said. "To see if it is really her sister, but apparently the tomb is already sealed. Do you know of any way she might get inside?"

His hand had moved from my belly back to my arm, running up and down, his fingers brushing my skin ever so gently.

"Possibly," he said at last. "I know someone who undertakes some rather disreputable jobs at times. He might be able to get her in."

"What kind of jobs?"

I felt the way he hesitated.

"Tell me," I said. "Please. I cannot decide if the risk is worth it if I don't know everything."

"Sometimes when a wealthy person has been interred, folk hire him to…" He hesitated again. I said nothing, only waited for him to continue. "They hire him to break into the tomb and steal any valuables he can carry out."

"He is a tomb robber?"

"You could call him that."

"This is a friend of yours?" I didn't know what to think. How could Khaemmalu be friends with someone so dishonourable?

His hand swept around my waist and up over my belly. It was hard to think with his fingers wandering my body.

"An acquaintance," he said. "I have known him since our school days."

"Why doesn't he…"

"Get an honest job?" he suggested when my voice trailed away. "He has one, but he also has five children, and honest work doesn't feed them all."

"I doubt Abar can pay for his services," I said. "But I can. Do you think he would accept a jewel in payment?"

"Certainly. Do you want to speak with your maid first, or should I talk to my acquaintance and see when he could take her there?"

"Would you check with him first? I would rather know he is willing before I tell her."

"I will see him as soon as I get off duty in the morning." Khaemmalu pressed his lips to the side of my neck. "But in the meantime, I can think of far more interesting things to do than talk about your maid."

It was only as I stifled a yawn some time later that Khaemmalu untangled his limbs from mine.

"It is late," he said. "And you can't be seen to be out all night."

He got to his feet and held out his hand to help me up, then wrapped his arms around my waist.

"We have to be very careful," he said. "We must both be entirely above suspicion if we are going to do this."

If we were going to have an affair, he meant. It was too late to think about such a thing after what we had done tonight. We had both broken the law about Pharaoh's Ornaments being reserved for his exclusive pleasure. And right now, I didn't even care. I set my palm against his cheek, thrilling in the feel of his skin beneath my hand. How wonderful it was to touch him like this, even if I could only do it in the dead of night, protected by the darkness and the shadows.

"Kassaya," he prompted when I didn't reply. "Tell me you understand the seriousness of this."

"I do," I whispered. "I just wish…"

He cut me off with a quick kiss.

"I know," he said. "I wish it too, but it won't do to talk about it. It is what it is, and we cannot change it."

With one last kiss, he grasped my shoulders and turned me around to face the other direction.

"Go now," he said. "Quickly."

"Will I see you tomorrow night?" I asked.

He stilled and my heart dropped.

"Oh," I said.

"No, you mistake me," he said quickly. "I want to, but we must avoid suspicion. Wait a couple of days before you come to find me again."

"How will you know which night I will come?"

"If you look for me, I will find you."

A flutter in my belly. The babe moving. I had to tell him.

"Khaemmalu—" I started.

"Go," he said. "Before someone finds us."

He gave my shoulders a little push and I started walking. I glanced back, hoping for one last glimpse before I left, but the darkness had already swallowed him.

I made my way back along the path in a daze. When Father first sent me to Egypt, I had hoped my husband would be a good and wise man, someone I could grow to love in time, or at least to care for. But from the first moment I saw Pharaoh, I knew that would never be the case.

The dismay I felt that day as I stood in the courtyard listening to him drone on about his own magnificence was still stark. He had kept us waiting for hours until he deigned to arrive, and for what? His speech contained nothing of importance. No significance whatsoever. It was no more than a lengthy accounting of how great he believed he was. I knew then he would never be someone I could love.

Whatever this was with Khaemmalu, I'd never expected to find it here in the Palace of the Ornaments where every woman Pharaoh claimed as his was forbidden to any other man. Where breaking the rules could result in a death sentence. But Khaemmalu was willing to risk it. For me. Surely that meant he loved me, even if he hadn't said the words. He risked his life for me in every moment we were together.

My footsteps slowed as the gravity of the situation sank in. Now I was away from Khaemmalu, I could think more clearly. Without his hands on my body and his lips on mine, I questioned my own wisdom and the soundness of my mind.

I saw how Tiye smirked as she talked about Hydna's affair with Weren. Such affairs might be strictly forbidden, but they were also viewed with some hilarity by the Ornaments. Or at least, that was the case when a woman had an affair with a modified man. I had been told the guards who patrolled the grounds weren't modified, and after tonight, I could certainly confirm that truth.

Was I mad to embark on such an affair? Knowing we would both lose our lives if we were discovered? It wasn't just myself I had to consider either. There was my son. If our affair was revealed, would he, too, pay the penalty for his mother's infidelity? Or would they wait until he was born before they carried out my sentence?

I might risk my own life, but not my son's. No matter what I felt for Khaemmalu, there could be nothing further between us.

CHAPTER 12

*A*hmose eventually let me in, although I had to knock twice. She yawned and looked more asleep than awake. My return had obviously woken her, although she had barred the door at some point after I left. She followed me to the bedchambers, where we parted without speaking.

I undressed and got into bed, expecting a restless night with my mind whirling as it was. But I must have fallen into a deep sleep because the next thing I knew was the bird singing its dawn song at my window. I lay there for a while, memories of Khaemmalu twirling through my mind. The way he kissed me, gentle at first, then with increasing passion. His hands running over me, the heat of his body against mine.

How could I stay away? When I wasn't with him, it felt like part of me was missing. Like the air I breathed was somehow less without his presence. Regardless of the risk, I didn't have it in me to end our affair, not even for the sake of my son.

It was only the warmth in the chamber that finally drew me from my bed. With the shutters still closed from the night, the air was heavy and hot. When I reached the sitting chamber, everyone except Ahmose was there.

"You slept very late." Ettu gave me a sharp look.

Not as late as Ahmose. I didn't say it, though. If she wasn't out of bed yet, then she hadn't told them I went out by myself, so Ettu had either guessed or she heard us talking last night. Maybe she heard my return. Either way, she clearly knew, so there was no point trying to pretend I hadn't.

"I couldn't sleep, so I went for a walk." I tried to sound nonchalant as I poured some melon juice. It slid down my throat, cool and sweet. I hadn't realised how thirsty I was. "I suppose it was rather late by the time I got back."

"Hmm," was all Ettu said.

"We sent your maids away," Merytre said. "We thought you must be ill."

Any day when I didn't have to endure the humiliation of sitting naked on the stool in my bathing chamber while ten women scrubbed and poked and prodded me was a good day.

"Never mind. I'm sure the three of you can manage well enough." I tried not to sound too cheery. If Ettu thought I lingered in bed to avoid my maids, she would be sure to come and rouse me the next time I lay in a little later.

The kitchen servants arrived with our morning meal and I was pleased for the distraction. By the time they had gone, and we had all served ourselves, I figured nobody was still thinking about my late night walk.

"Are you going to visit with Lady Tiye today?" Ettu asked a little later as she scraped the last of the gruel from her bowl.

"I should," I said. "I haven't seen her for a few days."

If any rumour already circulated about a guard having an affair with an Ornament, Tiye would know. I was certain she would mention it too. She had been quick to tell me when she heard about Hydna's affair with Weren.

Ettu only nodded and said nothing further. But as she and Sehener accompanied me to Tiye's chambers a little later, she made it clear she hadn't forgotten my late night excursion.

"You could have woken me last night." Ettu's tone was cool, which always indicated a problem. "I would have accompanied you when you went out."

"There was no need. You know the grounds are well patrolled at night."

"Indeed."

I pretended I didn't notice the sideways glance she gave me. Clearly, she wondered whether I'd seen Khaemmalu last night. I waited for her to ask, but thankfully she said nothing further. At least Sehener didn't ask anything. I would never keep a thing to myself if they both interrogated me at once, and the newness of whatever this was with Khaemmalu was something I wanted to hold onto for a little longer yet.

Ettu and Sehener waited at the end of Tiye's hallway. When I knocked on her door, it was Nammu who let me in. I hadn't seen her in Tiye's chambers for some time, and hadn't spoken to her since our encounter in the hallway. She had accused me of being pleased Ishtar was gone. Nammu smirked, a clear indication she hadn't forgotten our last conversation. I ignored her and swept past.

To my surprise, Tiye already had another visitor. Her expensive gown and elaborate wig told me she was an Ornament, although I was sure I'd never seen her face before. But in a place the size of the Palace, there must be many Ornaments I hadn't so much as seen, let alone met.

"Kassaya." Tiye's voice was warm, and if it bothered her I arrived while she already had a guest, she hid it well. "Do come sit down. Do you know Hydna?"

The woman sitting opposite Tiye gave me a nod and the whisper of a smile. So, this was the woman having an affair with the butler. She was quite pretty, with her features signalling she was of Egyptian heritage, although her skin was a little lighter than was usual. Perhaps one of her parents was from elsewhere. Like me, she surely knew the consequences of an affair. Did it make her hesitate? Had she ever resolved to break off her affair, but then found herself drawn irrevocably back to him?

"Well met," Hydna said to me.

I returned the greeting and hesitated, wondering where I was supposed to sit. Tiye and Hydna occupied a pair of couches which faced each other, and each sat in the middle of their couch. I needn't have worried, though, because Tiye, as usual, missed nothing. With a soft clearing of her throat and an inclination of her head, she indicated Hydna was to move over. Hydna, however, rose.

"I shall leave you to your next visitor," she said.

If she was annoyed at cutting her visit short, she gave no sign of it, only nodded at me again and left without further comment. Nammu had already planted herself in a chair and made no move to get up, so it was Bennerib who rushed to open the door. I settled myself in the spot Hydna had vacated. The cushion was still warm from her body.

"A busy morning for you," I said to Tiye.

She gave me an amused look. "So it would seem."

"I have not met her before, although I'm sure you have mentioned her."

I hoped my comment might prompt Tiye to tell me more about the affair. After all, she made it clear she found the situation both amusing and bewildering. Amused a woman would stoop to be with a modified man and bewildered as to the point of their affair if he couldn't get a child on her.

After being with Khaemmalu last night, I was beginning to understand the pleasure of an affair, whether the man was modified or not. If the butler did the sort of things to Hydna that Khaemmalu did to me—

My cheeks were already hot as I cut off my thought and returned my attention to Tiye. She arched her eyebrows at me, a clear indication she hadn't missed my blush. If she had never been with any man other than Pharaoh, she couldn't possibly understand. Pharaoh was no more skilled as a lover than he was at *senet*. Did Tiye even know what she was missing out on?

"I'm sure I have mentioned her," she said.

This would be the perfect time for her to mention the rumour of another affair if there was any new gossip, but Tiye only leaned back and sighed.

"Something troubling you?" I asked.

Not that I needed to. She would tell me if she wanted to, and if she didn't, then asking served no purpose anyway. She had probably already decided how much to share with me.

"I am concerned about Henutmire," she said at last. "Her father seems determined to provoke Pharaoh."

"She told me her father wrote," I said. "Something about wanting a letter from Henutmire."

"Apparently he suspects Henutmire may have gone to the West and Pharaoh has neglected to tell him."

"Why would he think such a thing?"

Tiye gave me a steady look.

"Rumours?" I guessed. "The number of women who go missing from here?"

"I suppose he is aware the letters he receives are not written by Henutmire's own hand, and he wants to be certain she still lives."

"He must love her very much."

Would my father ever do such a thing? Would he risk the alliance with Egypt for proof I lived? I hadn't yet written to tell him about Ishtar. He would want to know. She was always his favourite, or at least, she was until she got herself with child to avoid being sent to Pharaoh. Father would be devastated at the news of her death. No, I couldn't tell him yet. I would wait until Half returned, as I had already decided. Only once I had definitive proof of her fate would I write to my father.

"He has sent a messenger now," Tiye said, drawing me from my thoughts.

"A messenger?"

"One of his officials. The man has demanded to see Henut-mire with his own eyes."

I couldn't imagine Pharaoh taking that well. It was a clear implication Henutmire's father thought he lied.

"Will Pharaoh allow it?" I asked.

Tiye scoffed. "Of course not. He was already furious with the repeated demands by letter. Now a messenger as well? It is a wonder he has not sent the fellow back in pieces."

I blinked at her, too shocked to reply.

"Would he do that?" I asked, eventually realising I needed to say something.

Tiye shrugged. "If he is angry enough. More likely it will be something less dramatic. The man's ear, perhaps, or a finger. A warning to Henutmire's father that he is in no position to make such a demand of Pharaoh."

"But he will not send the messenger home?"

"I don't think so. He will want to make a point of the fact that Pharaoh, and Pharaoh alone, determines what comes to pass here. Of course, he hasn't met with the messenger yet. He might not even allow the man to present his message."

"And what of Henutmire?" I asked. "Will there be any punishment for her for her father's actions?"

His insolence, I supposed, was how Pharaoh would see it.

"I don't know," Tiye said with a heavy sigh. "That is what I am concerned about."

CHAPTER 13

By the time I left Tiye, it was too late to catch Henutmire in the dining chamber. I must remember to eat there tomorrow morning. She already knew her father had sent messages about her, but did she know Pharaoh had taken offence to them?

Ettu and Sehener chatted between themselves on the short walk back to my chambers, and I thought they hadn't noticed my distraction. But, of course, Ettu did.

"My lady?" She paused as she went to knock. "You are very quiet. Did Lady Tiye say something to upset you?"

"It is nothing," I said.

She flashed me a sharp look. I should have just said I was tired. That would have been no surprise after my late night.

"Henutmire's father has sent a messenger to ask after her," I said.

"I assume Pharaoh isn't pleased?" Ettu asked.

"Tiye didn't say," I said. "Only that he was angry about the letters."

"Will you warn her?" Sehener asked. "Perhaps she could tell her father he risks…"

Her voice trailed away, but I was sure we all knew what she tried to avoid saying. That Henutmire could be in danger if her father angered Pharaoh enough.

"He risks alienating an important ally," Ettu said quickly. She rapped on the door. "And that is something no man wants to do."

Merytre let us in, and soon Ettu and Sehener were immersed in some gossip she had heard from Sutem about one of the kitchen maids. I sat back in my chair and tried to look like I listened. I laughed when they did, but heard nothing of whatever it was the maid had done.

Henutmire might not even know of the danger to herself. There was no way to predict how Pharaoh might react. Look how he responded when I failed to answer a question from him. I needed to warn her. I regretted not warning Ishtar, even though it wouldn't have saved her, and I had withheld information from Hilde as well. I wouldn't make the same mistake again. The chatter around me died as I got up.

"I am going to visit with Henutmire," I said.

"You intend to warn her." Ettu was already on her feet, ready to accompany me.

Merytre looked from me to her.

"Warn her?" she asked. "Of what?"

I ignored the question and went to the front door. Ettu followed me.

"I will come with you," she said. "Sehener can tell the others what happened."

I waited while Tall slipped away to his bedchamber, then Ettu and I set off. I had only been to Henutmire's chambers once before and wasn't sure I could find them again, but Ettu didn't hesitate. I waited for her to comment, knowing it was unlikely she would keep her thoughts to herself.

When her footsteps slowed, I took it as an indication we had almost reached Henutmire's chambers and she was trying to figure out what to say in the few moments we had left.

"Just say it," I said. "You know it will make no difference, but you will feel better for having said it."

"Do you remember what happened when you pushed Lady Henutmire to tell you whether Pharaoh had ever hurt her?" she asked.

"She didn't want to tell me," I said.

"She was very upset you kept asking."

"She was afraid. I'm sure she had her reasons for not wanting to tell me."

Perhaps because she wasn't certain I wouldn't go straight to the administrators with what I knew. I hoped that wasn't the case. I thought I'd shown Henutmire she could trust me.

"Do you really want to upset her like that again?" Ettu asked.

We stopped just short of the door which I assumed was Henutmire's. Ettu's gaze held a challenge. I couldn't help admiring her as she stood there, her back straight and her head held high, dressed as no other woman dared to. It seemed so easy to be her. She wore what she wanted, said what she thought, and if anyone laughed or mocked her, she merely walked away.

"How do you do it?" I asked.

"Do what?" The look she gave me was puzzled, as if she honestly didn't know what I meant.

"Be…" I gestured towards her, realising I didn't have the words to explain my thought. "Be you."

"Me? I am nobody special. Just a lady's maid. But you." It was her turn to gesture at me now. "I am constantly in awe of you. You always do what your heart tells you is right, even when everyone says you are wrong. I wish I had your courage."

I was so surprised, I could only blink at her. If it was anyone else who said such a thing, I might have thought they lied, but Ettu was always unhesitating with the truth. I was so used to comparing myself to my sister and finding myself inferior, it had never occurred to me someone might admire me for what I was, rather than find me wanting for who I wasn't.

"This is Lady Henutmire's chambers," Ettu said. "Might I suggest…"

"Go on," I prompted when she stopped.

"Be gentle," she said. "I know you mean well, but she might not take kindly to your warning, especially if she thinks you are trying to interfere in her father's relationship with Pharaoh. Or her own." She added the last almost as an afterthought.

"I will."

She crouched to straighten my skirt. Fussing like this seemed to be Ettu's way of showing affection. I never quite knew what to do when she did such a thing and ended up frozen in place, waiting for her to finish. Apart from Tall and Half, I'd never had a friend before, and certainly not a female friend.

As I knocked on Henutmire's door, I glanced over my shoulder to see Ettu leaning against the wall, clearly settling in to wait. The door opened and a maid peered out at me. I vaguely recognised her face — she often attended Henutmire in the dining chamber — although I didn't know her name. She obviously knew me, though, and shot a look back over her shoulder, as if judging whether she should let me in.

Before I could speak, she sighed and opened the door wider. I entered the chamber and she was swift to close the door behind me.

Henutmire sat on a couch with her face buried in her hands. As the door closed, she looked up. It was only then I realised she was crying.

"Oh, Kassaya," she said between sobs. "The most terrible thing has happened."

I hurried over to sit beside her.

"Henutmire, whatever is the matter?" I asked.

She hiccuped and seemed to stifle a sob. Her maid brought a cloth and Henutmire allowed the woman to wipe her face. Her cheeks bore dark streaks of kohl and her maid's attempts at removal seemed to only smudge them. Henutmire waved her away and the maid departed with a frown, clearly dissatisfied with the state of her mistress's face.

"Pharaoh has sent for me," Henutmire said, giving me a look that seemed filled with both sorrow and terror.

I stammered as I tried to find an appropriate response. How much did she know? When Nebtu disappeared, Henutmire was genuinely distressed, but gave no sign of suspecting Pharaoh might be responsible. But when I asked if Pharaoh had ever hurt her, she refused to answer and seemed afraid to even discuss such a thing with me. She told me she had only been with Pharaoh twice, so I didn't know whether she had experienced his abuse for herself, or if she knew someone who had. Was she crying because she was afraid of him, or was there some other reason I couldn't guess at?

"Is that not a good thing?" I patted her knee, hoping the touch would soothe her. "Henutmire, of all the Ornaments, he has called for you this time."

She buried her face in her hands.

"You don't understand," she said.

I leaned over, trying to make out the words between her sobs.

"He is angry about Father's letters. He didn't summon me to bed me. He wants to punish Father."

My mind whirled as I tried to figure out what I could say to calm her. But whatever I said, it wouldn't be true. Pharaoh was certainly vindictive enough to take out his anger towards Henutmire's father on her. Did she know about the messenger, though, or only the letters?

I hesitated, wondering if I should keep what I knew to myself since she was already afraid. But I had come to tell her and now it was even more important that I did. I couldn't let her go to Pharaoh without knowing. I would not make the same mistake a third time.

My hesitation must have alarmed her, because Henutmire stopped sobbing and looked up at me. Her eyes were swollen and her kohl was smudged all over her cheeks.

"What is it?" she asked. "You know something."

"I spoke with Tiye earlier today."

Her eyes widened and she covered her mouth with her hand.

"Tell me," she said. "Quickly. I have not seen her since yesterday, so if something has happened, I know nothing of it."

"Your father sent a messenger."

"A messenger?" She frowned at me. "Father sent someone? Here?"

"To ask after you. Since Pharaoh hasn't responded to his letters."

"Oh, no." She put her face back in her hands. "That makes it even worse. Pharaoh must be furious."

"I don't think Tiye knows much more than that."

Or if she did, she wasn't saying.

"Tell me exactly what she said," Henutmire begged.

"That your father was trying to provoke Pharaoh and she was surprised the messenger wasn't returned to him in pieces."

Henutmire sat back with a heavy sigh.

"If…" Her voice trailed off and I waited, restraining my urge to prod her to continue. "If something happens to me, will you make sure my father knows? Send him a message, but not through Pentau. Send it however you got the message out to Nebtu's father."

Was it possible she didn't know the truth about the women who disappeared? That they fought against Pharaoh instead of submitting to him. She had clearly figured out he was responsible, but she didn't know the details. Why hadn't Tiye told her? I thought they were friends.

"Henutmire—" I stopped and swallowed down the words. Tiye did nothing without a reason. Maybe she thought ignorance would somehow protect Henutmire. Maybe there was more I didn't know myself.

"What?" she asked.

The tearful way she looked at me strengthened my resolve. Tiye might have her reasons for not warning a friend, but that didn't obligate me to do the same.

"There is something you should know," I said. "Before you see Pharaoh."

She wiped her face with the cloth, although it only served to smudge the streaks even further.

"Tell me," she said. "You told me once I could trust you. Prove it."

I cast my gaze around the chamber as I searched for the right words. Her accommodations looked much like everyone else's. Finely-made furniture, exquisite decorations. We lived in luxury, to be sure, but it hid dark secrets.

"The women who disappear…" I swallowed hard. Henutmire

wasn't the first person I had told. Why did it seem so much harder this time?

Henutmire watched me carefully. The way she held herself suggested she already knew something of what I wanted to tell her.

"Pharaoh is responsible." My words came out in a rush.

Henutmire's face didn't change. She went very still, as if waiting for more before she decided how to react.

"For their disappearance," I said.

Still she studied me. I couldn't decide whether she already knew or not.

"He needs them to believe they won't survive," I added. "If he puts his hands to your throat, it's very important you don't fight him."

Still nothing. She blinked at me, and had stopped crying, but she said nothing.

"Henutmire, do you understand what I'm saying? You must not fight back. If you do, you will be just another woman who disappears without trace. Another woman the administrators will claim returned to her father."

She nodded, although her face still didn't give any hint of what she thought.

"I suspected," she said at last. "Some of it, at least."

"Why didn't you tell me what you knew?" I asked.

"Likewise, you could have told me."

We both had our reasons and it didn't matter anymore. We both knew the truth.

"Is there more to it?" I asked. "Is there more I don't yet know?"

She seemed to hesitate.

"I know about Tiye's plan," I said, suspecting the reason for her hesitation.

Henutmire's face relaxed.

"That is all I know then," she said. "We will hold him responsible for his deeds. We will take the throne from him and put a better man in his place."

I waited, but if she knew Tiye had asked me to join them, she didn't say.

"Be careful," I said. "And would you send one of your maids to me after you return? I should like to know you are back safe."

She gave me a tight smile.

"You, Kassaya, are a true friend," she said. "And that is very rare in a place like this."

I left soon after. There was nothing else to say. I had told her what I knew, and I prayed to Marduk it would help keep her safe, but if not, at least not warning her wouldn't be another regret. I had failed both my sister and Hilde. I hadn't failed Henutmire.

Back in my chambers, I sought a reprieve from the chatter of the others. I lay in my bed and closed my eyes, but worry for Henutmire kept me awake. At least this time, my conscience was easy. If Pharaoh hurt her, she had the knowledge she needed to save herself. If only I had known that much before Ishtar went to him that last time.

A strong fragrance tickled my nose, making me sneeze. The scent of frankincense, just the same as the other day. But when I opened my eyes, I was still alone in my bedchamber.

I didn't feel alone, though. The aroma lingered, as if its wearer stood right beside my bed.

"Ishtar?" I whispered, and immediately felt like a fool.

Of course, my sister wasn't here. It was probably just a scent blowing in through the open windows, come from somewhere out in the Palace grounds. I closed my eyes again, determined to sleep, and tried to ignore the certain feeling that somebody else was indeed in my bedchamber.

CHAPTER 15

I finally fell asleep and passed the afternoon in an uneasy doze. It was only the increasingly urgent pressure in my bladder that finally drove me from my bed. As I reached my doorway, I came face-to-face with Ettu.

"Oh, you are up," she said. "I was coming to check on you. Are you unwell?"

"Just tired," I said.

She studied me with a frown, clearly not believing me.

"It is not like you to spend the whole afternoon in bed," she said. "Are you sure you are not ill? Perhaps we should send for a healer."

"I am well enough. Really," I added, when she continued to eye me with a dubious expression. "Did anyone come into my chamber while I was sleeping?"

Her expression became puzzled.

"I don't believe so," she said. "We were all in the sitting chamber the whole afternoon, except for once or twice when someone went to use the chamber pot. Why do you ask?"

"I thought someone came in," I said. "I must have dreamed it."

"Hmm," was her only reply.

The kitchen servants brought our evening meal and I tried to immerse myself in conversation. The scent of frankincense lingered with me, as did the certainty that someone had been in my bedchamber.

As the evening wore on, I found myself increasingly unable to sit still. I tried to pretend it was a result of lying in bed all afternoon and nothing to do with my longing to see Khaemmalu.

"Do you fancy a walk this evening?" Ettu asked.

I guessed she had noticed my restlessness.

"Yes, it is rather stuffy in here," I said.

It wasn't untrue. We always closed the shutters as dusk approached, bringing with it the incessant biting insects, and even now the days were cooler, it still left the chamber a little too warm for comfort.

"Merytre, you should come too," I said. "Sutem will be waiting for you anyway."

"I don't mind waiting until you go to bed if you would prefer," Merytre said, although the look on her face said she would very much like to be with Sutem.

"I hardly have any need of maids in the evening," I said. "There is no point you sitting here just for the sake of it."

Our conversation was interrupted by a loud yawn from Ahmose.

"Forgive me," she said. "I find myself so tired, I forgot my manners."

"You should go to bed," Sehener said quickly. "I can sit up until my lady and Ettu return."

Ahmose must have been tired indeed, because she didn't protest, only got to her feet and shuffled out of the chamber.

"Does she seem tireder than usual?" Ettu asked after Ahmose's door closed.

"She has been rather pale," Sehener said.

"She has hardly left these chambers for ages," Merytre added.

"She used to go out every day or two, but now she spends all day in either her chair here or in bed."

I tried to remember the last time Ahmose had gone out. She went to see her contact recently, the one who was liaising with the librarian, Messui, for us. I couldn't remember how many days ago that had been. I had been so absorbed in everything else that was happening, I'd lost track of time. I assumed Ahmose would let me know if she learned anything useful, so it hadn't seemed necessary to spend time wondering about it.

"She is an old woman," I said. "It isn't unusual to be tired at her age."

I never knew my mother's mother, but my father's mother had been an old woman when I was a girl. I remembered little about her other than that she fell asleep every time she sat down. Ahmose was probably even older than her, so it was no surprise if she tired easily. The woman must be fifty years, at least.

Ettu, Merytre and I left. Sehener barred the door behind us and I didn't miss the furtive glance between her and Tall. I guessed they would find a way to occupy themselves while we were gone.

Outside, the air was cool and a light breeze brought the scent of flowers. I inhaled deeply, searching for any trace of frankincense, but the pollens made my nose stuffy and then I couldn't smell anything at all.

We set off and had barely reached the first spot where bushes lined the path before a rustling alerted me to Khaemmalu's presence. He didn't speak, perhaps not wanting to reveal himself to my companions.

"Keep walking," I said and slipped away into the bushes.

Ettu huffed, but a quiet murmur from Merytre forestalled any comment. As the shadows surrounded me, Khaemmalu's fingers found my hand. He led me through the shrubbery.

"I hoped to see you tonight," he said, stopping in a clearing which was barely large enough for us both to stand in.

"Me too." It felt like a daft thing to say and my cheeks heated. At least he wouldn't see my blush in the darkness.

He moved closer and his arms slid around my waist. I raised my hands to his chest, my fingers tracing the firm muscles beneath his linen shirt. His mouth claimed mine and, for a time, there were no thoughts in my head.

Some time later, we were lying together in the grass. My discarded gown was draped over a nearby bush and Khaemmalu's fingers traced a path up and down my arm.

"Before I forget," he said. "I spoke to my friend. The one you thought was dishonourable."

"I never called him that."

"But you thought it." His voice was teasing. "Didn't you?"

"Maybe." I snuggled in closer so he wouldn't be tempted to take offence.

"He can get your maid into the tomb," Khaemmalu said. "But he cautions against it, even knowing you offered a gem in payment. So, he cannot be all that dishonourable if he would turn down such riches."

"Why won't he take her?"

"Because he thinks it would be too traumatic for a young woman to bear, and if the body has been preserved, your maid won't recognise her sister anyway. She will be wrapped in linens, and there is too much risk of damage to unwrap them. If your maid hopes to view the body to convince herself it is really her sister, I'm afraid that won't be possible."

I sighed. "I thought it might give her some comfort if she knew with certainty it was her sister."

He kissed my jaw, then feathered more kisses down my neck.

"I don't really want to talk about your maid right now," he said.

And for a while, we didn't speak again.

"Remember that day you went sailing?" he murmured in my ear some time later. "And the boat overturned?"

"Of course I do."

How could anyone forget that day? We would never know whether it was merely a stray gust of wind or a magic spell that tipped the boat on which we sailed. Kia and a serving woman lost their lives to the water that day.

"I never told you how much I admired you," he said. "The other women were panicking and crying, but not you. Pharaoh would have drowned long before anyone got to him if you hadn't been there to keep him afloat."

"I wish I had been able to find Kia sooner," I said. "I looked for her."

"We all wish things had occurred differently, but that day would have had a vastly different ending if you hadn't done what you did."

If I had known then what I now knew about Pharaoh, would I have still helped save him? Or would I have swum to shore, leaving him to drown before his guards reached him? I didn't have an answer for that. The only thing I knew for certain was that if he had drowned that day, my sister would still be alive.

"Can I ask you something?" I caught Khaemmalu's fingers, revelling in the feeling of being able to hold them.

"Of course." His lips nuzzled my neck.

"What do you know about Amankhau?"

"The administrator?"

"Mmm." His lips on my shoulder were distracting and I tried to focus on my question. "I don't trust him."

"Why not?"

His mouth left my shoulder. My eyes had adjusted enough to the darkness to see he raised his head and studied me. I hesitated, not wanting to sound foolish. Everyone knew I had reason to dislike Amankhau and I worried Khaemmalu might think it no more than that. When I didn't reply, he nudged me with his shoulder.

"Tell me, Kassaya," he said.

"Every time a woman disappears, Amankhau seems to be involved," I said, although still reluctantly.

His fingers which had been twining around mine froze and his body stiffened. He drew away slightly, but then seemed to realise and came back to press himself against my side.

"What have you heard?" he asked.

"You know the administrators always say a missing woman has gone back to her father's home, or that she has run off with a lover."

"Of course."

"The thing is, they always seem to disappear at night. It is always Amankhau who says they chose to leave. Never Panouk. When I asked Panouk about it, he said Amankhau was trustworthy and appointed by Pharaoh himself."

"You have clashed with Amankhau several times," he said.

"I have, and I fear that if he is involved, it might make me a target. It would be convenient for him if I disappeared."

"I have never liked him." Khaemmalu spoke slowly and I could feel him putting the pieces together. "Nor do I trust him, but if I ever wondered whether he was involved, I would have thought I was letting my distaste for him influence me. He is a strange man, to be sure, quick to anger, and with a reputation for summoning the healers over even the slightest ailment. The healers quite despise him, because he refuses to believe them when they say there is nothing wrong with him."

It surprised me to learn Amankhau was not as invincible as he pretended to be. I would have expected him to be the type to stolidly persist in his duties, no matter how unwell he felt.

"We know women disappear from both palaces, so someone in authority here must be involved," I said.

"Nobody disappears from here." His voice was absent, as if he spoke without thinking.

"Of course they do," I said. "I have heard about men dragging women from their chambers."

I felt, rather than saw, him shake his head.

"I have heard the rumours myself, but it isn't true," he said. "And nobody leaves without the night guards knowing. I myself would know. If an Ornament is expected to go out, we always have advance notice. We know exactly who will be leaving, and when, and how."

"But that means…" My voice trailed away. We had been looking in the wrong place all this time. Amankhau probably wasn't involved after all.

"They always disappear after being summoned by Pharaoh. That doesn't mean Amankhau is innocent, though," he continued, as if guessing my thoughts. "If a woman is to leave the grounds at night, Amankhau has to approve it. The authorisation for the gate guards always comes from him."

We were silent for a few moments. I was busy trying to adjust my thoughts to slot in this new information. Beside me, Khaem-malu shifted and I felt his unease.

"Kassaya, there is something I haven't told you," he said.

Me too, I wanted to say.

"About my wife's disappearance," he added.

"Tabiry?"

He had said little about her, only that one night she didn't return from her job in Pharaoh's palace and was never seen again.

"She had recently come to Pharaoh's attention." He spoke reluctantly, as if this was something he didn't want to admit, even to himself. "Pharaoh summoned her the night she disappeared."

"Bebi told you?"

"Yes."

"Why didn't you tell me earlier?"

He gave a heavy sigh.

"We kept that detail quiet," he said. "Only those in Pharaoh's personal squad who were on duty that night know."

"But why keep it a secret?"

"Because I couldn't bear to think of what it meant for Tabiry." His voice was very quiet now. "Of what she suffered."

"You told me you went to the palace and asked for her when she didn't come home," I said.

"I did, but I wasn't able to speak with Bebi until the next day. He knew Pharaoh had summoned her that night, but he didn't know she never left." He hesitated, and I waited. It felt like there was more he wanted to say. "It wasn't the first time he called for her. Apparently it had happened twice before."

"She didn't tell you?"

He pressed his face into my neck and shook his head. His breath shuddered when he inhaled.

"She didn't know what we knew," he said. "About the women who disappear after meeting with Pharaoh. How we believe his captain and second cover for him. I kept it from her. I didn't want to worry her, and there are thousands of workers at the palace. I didn't think she would ever encounter him, let alone draw his attention in that way."

I hardly knew what to say.

"Why didn't you tell me?" I asked.

He was silent for a long while. I waited, letting him sort through his thoughts.

"I wasn't a very good husband to her," he said. "I failed her when she needed me the most and that shames me. I should have protected her."

"Do you ever wonder..." My voice trailed away. I shouldn't ask.

"Wonder what?"

"Whether things might have been different if you had told her?"

Like I wondered whether Ishtar's fate might have changed if she knew we suspected Pharaoh was responsible for the women who disappeared. But Khaemmalu didn't know the one piece of information that might have saved Tabiry back then.

That she shouldn't fight back. And I didn't know it in time to save Ishtar.

"Not a day has passed that I don't regret not sharing my suspicions with her," Khaemmalu said. "If she knew, she would have told me he had called for her. I could have stopped her from going to him. Sent her away. I could have kept her safe."

I couldn't tell him what I knew. It would only worsen his regret.

CHAPTER 16

I left Khaemmalu, although not without wishing I didn't have to. As I reached the path again, I spotted Ettu. Beside her walked a small figure shrouded in blankets. My heart leaped. It must be Half. And if he had returned, it meant news of Ishtar. I couldn't stop myself from hoping he brought information to prove we were wrong. That Ishtar was safe after all.

The blankets so completely shrouded Half that I could see nothing of him and he surely couldn't see out either, although Ettu guided him with an arm around his shoulders.

"Quickly," she whispered. "We need to get him inside."

We turned back towards the Palace. As we approached the front doors, my heart pounded. If it was Karpusa and Khaemope who guarded the doors, I would feel less anxious. They had shown no curiosity in anyone who accompanied me, whether they could identify the person or not. But I barely knew the night guards and couldn't even remember their names.

Their gazes flicked over me as we approached, but if they looked at Half at all, I didn't see it. I gave them a cheery "good evening" as they held the doors open for us. Then we were inside the Palace.

"We should walk more slowly," Ettu murmured. "We look like we are hurrying."

I slowed my pace, albeit reluctantly. Right now, I wanted nothing more than to get back to the safety of my chambers and find out what Half had learned. My heartbeat pounded my sister's name. Ishtar, Ishtar, Ishtar. She might be alive. She might have left after all. No, don't think it, I chastised myself. There is no possibility. You know that. Ishtar, drummed my heart.

We made our way up the stairs. One flight and we hadn't encountered anyone who would question us. Two flights. We were just about to start up the final flight of stairs, when I spotted Amankhau coming down the hallway. Of course it would be him. Panouk would have gone off duty as the sun set, leaving Amankhau in charge of the Palace overnight.

"Go," I whispered. "Quickly. We cannot afford to be stopped by him."

We quickened our pace, but it was too late.

"Lady Kassaya."

I pretended I didn't hear him as we made our way up the final set of stairs.

"Lady Kassaya," he called. "I must insist you stop."

I held my head high and kept going.

"Stop at once." His voice was shrill now. He wasn't going to let me walk away.

"Go," I whispered. "Lock the door and do not open it until I return."

As Ettu and Half hurried the rest of the way up, I turned back to Amankhau who had reached the bottom of the stairs.

"Administrator." I made my voice as pleasant as possible and prayed it gave no hint of how much I despised him. "Is there a problem?"

"Who was that?" he asked.

"My lady's maid?" I gave him a bland smile and feigned ignorance. "That was Ettu. I'm sure you have met her previously. She travelled with me from Babylon."

I was tempted to remind him about how he imprisoned Ettu when she was falsely accused of stealing a jewel belonging to Tiye. It might distract him if I could provoke an argument.

"Not her," he said rather impatiently. "The other one."

"The other one, Administrator?" I raised my eyebrows at him and forced my mouth into a smile. "I'm afraid I don't know what you mean."

It was a hopeless ploy and I wasn't even sure why I said it. Amankhau was not the type who would be dissuaded merely because I pretended not to know what he was talking about. But now I had played that hand, I had to keep up the pretence.

"The other person," he snapped. "The one wrapped in blankets."

"Blankets? Administrator, I confess I'm quite puzzled. I don't know what you are referring to."

"The other person with your woman," he said. "The little one."

Khaemmalu's comments about Amankhau summoning the healers suddenly became valuable information.

"Administrator, do you feel quite well?" I asked, making my way back down the stairs to him. "Perhaps it is the heat. It has been rather hot of late. May I suggest you retire to your bedchamber? It would seem you are in need of rest."

"I don't need rest," he snapped. "I demand to know who the other person is."

"Should I call for a healer? Or a physician? I fear the heat has quite addled your brain."

"Don't be ludicrous. I know what I saw."

"I believe an excess of heat can cause hallucinations." I kept my voice even as I feigned concern for him. "Perhaps I should summon a healer. Do sit down. Let me find a runner boy and I will send for a healer immediately."

"You are being absurd," he said. "I feel quite well."

But he didn't sound so sure any more.

"Administrator, sit down," I urged. "You can rest against the wall here. I will find a runner immediately."

I didn't let myself look back as I hurried away from him. He didn't call after me, so I could only pray to Marduk he had bought my story. I went straight to my chambers. Sehener opened the door when I knocked.

"Did he—" she started, but I waved away her question.

"Go find a runner," I said. "Amankhau is sitting in the hallway at the bottom of the stairs, or at least he was when I left. Tell the boy to send a healer to urgently attend to the administrator. The heat has addled his brain and he is imagining things."

She raised her eyebrows and gave me an impressed look.

"Go," I repeated. "Quickly."

She hurried away down the hallway. In the men's bedchamber, Half perched on his bed. Ettu sat beside him, clutching his hand and looking remarkably composed. Any other woman might have burst into tears at the unexpected return of the man she loved, but then, Ettu was like no other woman I knew. Tall sat opposite them on his own bed.

"Where is Ahmose?" I asked, surprised she wasn't here to hear Half's news.

"She felt light-headed and has gone to lie down," Ettu said.

Her voice was as calm as ever and gave no hint of the relief she must surely feel at Half's return. I studied him, unsure of what to ask first. Did I ask if he was well, or if he had news of Ishtar, or if anyone had seen him who shouldn't have, or whether he encountered Userhet who stabbed him, or…

"Princess." Half inclined his head towards me. "I have the information you sent me to find. About your sister."

My heart felt like it stopped, and for a few moments, I forgot to breathe. Ishtar, Ishtar, Ishtar pounded my heart when it started again.

Someone knocked and Ettu jumped up to answer the door. I

heard a brief conversation before the sitting chamber door opened. Maybe she had been checking Sehener was alone, since we hadn't locked the men's door.

"Perhaps we should sit out here," Ettu called from the sitting chamber. "We will all be more comfortable."

By the time I got there, Tall had already moved a footstool over to the couch Half usually sat on, and he climbed up to his seat. He sat there, his legs swinging a little, with Ettu at his side, once again clutching his hand.

She had a fierce look on her face, as if she had decided she would never let him go anywhere without her again. She told me once she didn't intend to take a husband, because she wanted to make her own way in the world. I wondered whether she had changed her mind.

"I encountered a healer before I found a runner," Sehener said. "And sent her straight to Amankhau."

I had almost forgotten why she had been gone. Amankhau and his suspicions had faded from my mind with the promise of news of Ishtar.

"Well, then," Ettu said before I could reply. She gave Half an expectant look. "Go on."

Half gave a heavy sigh, then looked me right in the eyes.

Ishtar, beat my heart, but sadly this time. His sigh had left me in no doubt as to the nature of his news.

"I am sorry to say there can be no uncertainty about your sister's fate," he said.

He been gone for some weeks. He didn't know we were all but certain already. Despite the fact this was the news I expected him to bring, tears prickled my eyes. I swallowed, unsure whether I would be able to speak if I tried, or if I would simply burst into tears. But Half didn't wait, only continued with his tale.

"I believe I know where her body is," he said.

My heart stuttered and the chamber tilted around me. For a moment or two, everything went black, but then I blinked and found myself on the couch, clutching its arm as if I was about to fall off.

I met Ettu's calm gaze. Sehener studied her hands as if she couldn't bear to look at me. Tall's face bore sympathy. Half watched me carefully, as if waiting for my reaction. I couldn't make myself speak, so I only nodded for him to continue.

"On the other side of the Great River," Half said, "is a place where tombs are cut into the rock. There is a special area where only those who have been pharaoh are interred, but not far from that is a location where queens and other noble women are placed. Your sister's body was taken there."

I hadn't expected any respect to be paid to her body. Not after the woman who was found abandoned in the quarry, and the one from the river, although we were never certain they weren't the same person.

"She was buried as a queen?" I asked.

"I am afraid not." Half's voice was gentle. "They opened a tomb, deposited her inside, and sealed it again. It seems they thought there was no chance she would ever be found, not in this lifetime at any rate."

"She was not…" My voice trailed away.

"She was not embalmed in the manner of the folk here, from what I have been able to determine," he said.

So, there was no respect for her body, after all. She was merely discarded like the other women we knew of. Trash to be disposed of, or hidden away.

These days, I felt like I straddled two cultures. I was no longer entirely Babylonian, but I also wasn't Egyptian. I wasn't even sure what I believed anymore. About the gods, the afterlife, about anything. However, as I examined my feelings, I realised I didn't care that her body hadn't been embalmed as the folk here preferred.

I didn't share their belief that a spirit needed its body kept intact. But I knew with deep certainty that a body had to be buried with the appropriate rites and prayers to keep the spirit in the afterlife. Ishtar had received none of the respect that should have been paid to her from either culture.

"I presume there are many tombs in this place?" Ettu asked.

"Hundreds," Half said. "But before you ask, yes, I believe I know exactly where she was taken."

Once again, they all looked at me. I waited for someone to speak, for an explanation of why they stared.

"What is it?" I asked finally.

"I suppose…" Ettu started.

"I thought…" Sehener added.

I waited, but nobody seemed inclined to reveal their thoughts.

"Tell me," I said, a little impatiently.

It was Ettu who finally said it.

"Since we know where Lady Ishtar's body was taken," she said, "I suppose we are wondering if you wish to retrieve her for a proper burial."

CHAPTER 17

*E*ttu knew as well as I did that if my sister had been entombed without the correct rites, her spirit might not stay in the afterlife. What spirit would willingly remain there in the dimness when they could make their way back to the world of the living? If we retrieved Ishtar's body, we could conduct the rites she should have been buried with.

But even if I could retrieve her, how would I find someone in Egypt who knew the proper burial rites? The correct prayers that should be said? I couldn't conduct such a ceremony, and I doubted Ettu or Half or Tall could either.

And what would I do with her body then? She should be buried where her family could bring offerings to her, where she would be near us, like under the floor of her father's home, but since Ishtar had been interred in a place of queens, maybe that was satisfactory to her. Besides, I couldn't imagine Panouk giving permission to bury her beneath the Palace. And without her body having been preserved, it was probably too late to try to send her back to Babylon. What captain would take such cargo on his ship?

As I worked through these thoughts, another realisation

crashed over me: I no longer had any reason to put off writing to my father. When Ishtar first disappeared, I didn't want to write to him because she might yet be found safe and well. Then once I knew she probably wouldn't be, I told myself I would wait until I was certain. Until her body had been found. Now there was no longer any excuse. I had to send that letter.

It all felt like too much and suddenly there was no air left in the chamber. I had to get out of there.

"I am going for a walk," I said, abruptly getting to my feet.

Ettu started to speak, presumably offering to come with me, but hesitated and I guessed she was reluctant to leave Half so soon.

"I will accompany you," Sehener said quickly.

Ettu shot her a grateful look. I was happy for her to stay behind anyway. Sehener would be far less likely to interrogate me while we walked.

Fortunately there was no sign of Amankhau as we made our way down the stairs. I could only pray to Marduk he believed me he was imagining things when he saw Half. Maybe we should get them out of the Palace tonight, before Amankhau had time to wonder whether he should inspect my chambers for signs of the person he thought he saw.

But how would we do that without Ahmose's special potion, and where would they go? Half surely had more to tell us. They couldn't leave. Not yet.

"This way." I pointed as we emerged outside.

It wasn't the direction I would normally go, along the path that meandered through the shadowy places where Khaemmalu was often to be found. I needed to think, to clear my head, and I wouldn't be able to do that with him. If he touched me, or he kissed me. Sehener interrupted my thoughts.

"My lady, are you well?" She gave me a curious look. "You are breathing rather oddly."

I pushed away thoughts of Khaemmalu's hands on my body.

"Perfectly," I said. "Perhaps we were just walking a little fast."

"Oh, we should slow down, then," she said.

I matched her leisurely pace and pretended that was why I had been breathing roughly. Sehener commented on the coolness of the night air and speculated on the species of bird we could hear somewhere off to our left, but must have felt like I rebuffed her attempts at conversation as she soon fell silent. As we reached the far end of the Palace, she tried again.

"We have walked quite a long way," she said. "Do you wish to turn back? You must be tired by now."

"Let's go a little further." My mind still whirled and I was no closer to any of the answers I sought.

Sehener only nodded and made no further comment. We followed the path around the end of the Palace. Some distance ahead of us lay the pleasure lake. I hadn't been there since the day Ishtar, Kia and I sailed with Pharaoh. The day a mysterious gust of wind overturned our boat and Kia drowned.

How strange that Khaemmalu should mention that day and then I found myself drawn towards the lake. But perhaps that was why I came this way, because it was on my mind after he had spoken of it.

As we approached the pleasure lake, Sehener seemed to hesitate.

"My lady," she said. "Are you sure you want to walk down here? Does it not bring back unpleasant memories?"

"It doesn't bother me." Ettu would know it was a lie, but I didn't think Sehener would, or at least, she wouldn't say it if she did. "I would like to walk along the edge of the lake."

As we strolled across the grassy expanse, it was hard not to think about the last time I was here. The day Ishtar and I sailed on the lake. The day the boat overturned. The day Kia and a servant woman drowned.

As we walked alongside the lake, the earthy scent of frankincense reached my nose.

"Do you smell that?" I asked.

Sehener obediently sniffed the air.

"The water?" she asked. "It does smell somewhat dank."

"No, the perfume."

She sniffed again.

"I don't think I'm smelling whatever you are," she said. "There aren't any flowers planted here, so something must be carrying on the breeze."

I let it drop. It was frankincense, I was sure of it. Just like the perfume Ishtar wore.

"Oh, it is muddy here," Sehener said.

She pointed, directing me around the mud. It was already too late for me. Cool mud squelched up the edges of my sandals and oozed along the side of my foot. As I tiptoed through it, my sandal landed on something hard. I stopped to pluck it from the mud, although later I couldn't have said why I did such a thing. It was most likely a rock.

The object I retrieved was indeed hard like rock, although it was curiously lumpy.

"What do you have there?" Sehener asked.

"I don't know."

I made my way across the bank and bent to wash the item in the lake. The mud was even deeper here and it seeped between my toes, cool and slimy.

It wasn't a rock at all, but wooden and no longer than the length of my thumb.

"A lioness," Sehener observed.

Of course it would be.

"I think it is Ineni's offering to Kia," I said. "From the farewell ceremony. She was going to throw our offerings in the lake."

"It must have washed back up," Sehener said.

We both turned to study the expanse of water. In the light of the crescent moon, it was dark and formless. It was deep too. That I knew from my efforts to locate Kia after the boat overturned. I had seen a flash of white somewhere down below, but she was too deep for me to reach.

It seemed unlikely such a tiny object tossed into the lake could have washed back up. Maybe it never reached the water. Perhaps Ineni dropped it before she could throw it in and wasn't able to find it again. That too seemed unlikely, but I couldn't think of any other explanation. No reasonable explanation anyway.

I repressed a shudder as I closed my fingers around the little wooden lion. They were everywhere. Lions and narcissus. What did they mean?

CHAPTER 18

$\mathcal{B}$ack in my chambers, everyone else had already gone to bed. At first, I was surprised they weren't waiting up for my return so Half could share whatever else he had learned. But then I realised it must be very late by now. He would be tired after walking all the way from Pharaoh's palace and I didn't even know how long he hid in the gardens before Ettu found him. I set the lioness on my dressing table and went to bed.

When I rose the next morning, my gaze went straight to the little figurine, which stood right where I left her. I had dreamed she moved during the night, although the images had faded now and I could barely recall them. As I headed out to the sitting chamber, I encountered Sehener emerging from her bedchamber.

The others were already up, Merytre had arrived, and they were all immersed in a merry conversation. Ettu and Half sat close together, their clasped hands between them. Tall's eyes brightened when he saw Sehener and he shifted a little on the couch, as if to make clear there was room for her beside him.

Ahmose was in her usual spot, resting with her head against the back of the chair and her eyes closed. I assumed they had already relayed Half's news about my sister to her. Perhaps that was the cause of her alarmingly pale face.

"Ahmose, are you well?" I asked.

She squinted at me and seemed to shake herself a little.

"Well enough," she said, sounding almost normal.

I sat on a couch and set the little lioness on the arm.

"What do you have there?" Ettu asked, leaning forward to look at it.

"I think it is the offering Ineni gave to Kia," I said. "At her farewell ceremony."

"Where did you find it?" she asked.

"Beside the pleasure lake."

"It was buried in the mud," Sehener offered. "My lady walked right over it."

"Why was it in the mud?" Ettu frowned as she glanced between me and Sehener.

I shrugged. "Ineni was going to throw it in the lake. That is all I know."

Ettu looked to Sehener, as if seeking more of an explanation from her, but Sehener only shrugged.

I studied the lioness for a while. Something about her puzzled me. Her sudden reappearance, perhaps, or the fact that this was yet another lion in my life. Eventually, I tucked her away in my pouch. There was something else I needed to turn my mind to today: the letter for my father.

Half had yet to share whatever else he had learned with us, but I didn't want to put off writing any longer. The more I waited, the more chance there was I would find yet another reason to delay.

Merytre and Sehener went to locate the scribe. I hoped he might return with them and give me a reason to avoid the usual bathing routine with my maids, but I was not so fortunate.

Pentau's sharp rap on the door a couple of hours later made me jump. Tall and Half were already safely locked away in their bedchamber in anticipation of the scribe's arrival, but every time someone knocked, I still feared it might be a messenger come to summon me to Pharaoh to account for running away from him.

Pentau didn't have the muscular physique that so many men here did. Rather, he was a small, skinny fellow with a sunken belly. As he arranged his little wooden table and his reeds, inks, and sheets of papyrus, I was still searching for the best way to relay Ishtar's death to my father. Kneeling in front of his table, Pentau finally gave me a nod to indicate he was ready to begin.

The women had all retreated to their bedchambers to give me some privacy while I dictated my letter. I wished one of them had stayed with me. I would have liked a sympathetic face to look at. Something other than the indifferent gaze Pentau gave me.

"To my father, Marduk-apla-iddina," I said. Pentau began his transcription, scratching swiftly at the papyrus with his reed. "Father, I write to tell you of the most grievous news. My dear sister—"

My throat choked and I stopped. While I waited for Pentau, I had only been thinking of what words to use. I hadn't considered how difficult it would be to say them, especially to someone who was practically a stranger to me.

Pentau gave me a stern look.

"Continue," he said, his voice absent of any sympathy, despite my obvious distress.

I ignored him and took a deep breath to steady myself.

"My dear sister, Ishtar," I said, then stopped again as I realised how little I could tell my father through Pentau. I could say only as much as the scribe would expect me to know, which was nothing more than that Ishtar had never returned from Pharaoh's palace.

Pentau shot me an impatient look and cleared his throat. It was an obvious signal he had better things to do than wait for me to find the right words.

"My dear sister, Ishtar, disappeared some weeks ago," I said.

"The administrators say she returned to Babylon, but I have received no word from her since. If she has returned home, I beg you write to me to confirm this. I miss her terribly and I fear for her safety. Your dutiful daughter, Kassaya."

Pentau's scribbling continued for some time after I finished my dictation. I refrained from asking what else he wrote, knowing it would only infuriate him. At length, he set down his reed, packed up his supplies, and got to his feet.

"Your letter will be sent with all reasonable haste," he said with something that might almost have been a bow if it wasn't so brief. "Good day to you."

Then he was gone, bustling out the door and down the hallway as if he had far more important duties to attend to.

The others quickly emerged from their bedchambers.

"Will your father understand?" Ettu asked as she barred the door.

They probably heard everything I said to Pentau.

"I don't see how he could from such a letter," I said. "He will most likely think she has run away."

He had good justification to do so, after all, given how Ishtar had done her best to avoid being sent to Egypt.

"If you need to send a secret letter," Ahmose said as she lowered herself into her chair, "I will obtain more of the special ingredient for my potion. It is risky, though. That butler is still asking too many questions."

Weren, she meant. The one having an affair with Hydna. How odd that someone with secrets of his own to hide would work so hard to uncover other people's secrets.

"Oh, no," Merytre said. "That is not necessary. I don't know why I didn't think of this before, but I can take your letter and see it to a courier."

"Of course." Relief flooded through me. I finally had an easy and legitimate way to get letters out without going through Pentau. Since Merytre now lived with Sutem, she had only to slip a letter into her pouch and carry it right out. In fact, I probably could have asked Khaemmalu, or even Sutem, to take a letter for me at any time. Both had shown willingness to break the rules for me. It seemed so obvious, but I never thought of it earlier.

"I will fetch your writing implements," Ettu said, already on her way out of the chamber.

Tall carried a table over to set it in front of me. Ettu laid out a sheet of papyrus, a little pot of ink, and a reed pen, then stepped back and looked at me expectantly.

"I can't think of what to say with you standing there staring at me," I said a little irritably.

She gave me a reproachful look, but retreated to sit beside Half. He reached for her hand, as if to comfort her, which only irritated me more. Why was everyone else able to be with the person they cared for? Ettu and Half had each other, and Merytre had Sutem. I didn't know what the situation was between Tall and Sehener, but they definitely seemed to like each other. Only Ahmose had nobody, but I supposed at her age, she didn't expect it anyway.

You are a princess, I reminded myself, and here to fulfil the terms of the alliance, not to fall in love. I pushed Khaemmalu's face out of my mind and turned my attention to my letter.

"Dear Father," I wrote. "You will receive a second letter from me via the palace scribe. He sends all official correspondence and everything that goes through him is censored. In truth, I do not even know what that letter will say, for I am not permitted to hear what he has written to you. This letter I send in secret and I beg that if you reply, you make no mention of it, for I am permitted to write only through the scribe. My other letter, the official one, tells you my dear sister has returned home. In truth, Father, she has been murdered."

Dare I tell Father it was Pharaoh himself who killed her? What impact would that have on the alliance between our countries? Perhaps nothing, given Ishtar was not the one sent in fulfilment of the treaty. Perhaps everything, because she was still our father's daughter, however furious he may have been with her.

If I told Father the truth, he might write directly to Pharaoh to accuse him. How would Pharaoh react to such a charge? Given his fury at the messages from Henutmire's father, I knew he wouldn't be pleased.

Also, it would be obvious that such information must have come from me and that I had sent an unauthorised letter. The administrators would question me, and that could lead to them searching my chambers for evidence of other broken rules. I couldn't risk it.

"I have received word through a friend that her body was deposited in a tomb in a nearby burial area," I wrote. "I know this letter will bring you and Mother much grief, and I regret that. I can only assure you that I join you in your grief. Your daughter, Kassaya."

I re-read the letter, wondering if I should start over. But it said everything I needed to, and if I let myself write it again, I'd spend all day trying to find the perfect way to tell my father. Once the ink was dry, I folded the papyrus and held it out to Merytre. She slipped it into her pouch.

"Either Sutem or I will make sure it gets into the hands of a courier tonight," she said.

Was I making a mistake in sending a second letter? Could I trust Father would take my warning not to reply seriously enough? I couldn't be sure, but he should know what happened to Ishtar. And if something happened to me, at least Father would know the truth about her disappearance and would have reason to suspect whatever the administrators told him. Surely no reasonable man would believe both of his daughters had fled, supposedly heading for home, only to never arrive.

CHAPTER 19

e sat in silence for some time after I finished the letter to my father.

"We have not yet heard all of Half's news," Ettu eventually pointed out.

"Of course," I said. "Half, what else have you to tell us?"

He swung his legs a little as he considered where to start.

"It was a difficult assignment, to be sure," he said. "Since my priority was to be seen as little as possible, I spent much time hidden away, waiting for the cover of dark and lateness before I ventured out."

It must have been lonely and frustrating for him, spending all day hidden away, likely in a dark place, with nobody to talk to and nothing but his own thoughts for company. He wouldn't even have anything to eat unless he had saved something from the previous night. And, of course, he would have to ensure he kept well clear of Userhet, the guard who had stabbed him. I hadn't really thought about what it would be like for him before. He had volunteered to go, but it was quite selfish of me to let him.

"Did Userhet see you?" Ettu asked, as if she knew what I was thinking.

"If he did, I never saw him," Half said. "Of course, he may well have heard I had returned, but thank Marduk, I never encountered him. There were others who saw me, though. Runner boys, kitchen maids, and the like. Those who are up and about in the dead of night. The kind of folk who have no reason to talk to one of Pharaoh's men."

He paused to clear his throat and Merytre jumped up.

"Let me fetch you some beer," she said. "I'm sure you still have much to tell us."

She was swift to press a mug into his hands and Half gave her a grateful nod. He took a long sip through the reed straw and sighed.

"Aah, that is better," he said. "Now, I spent the first few days creeping through the hallways, listening at doors and hiding around corners to hear what folk said when they encountered each other. I heard nothing but the most mundane things, and quickly realised I would gain no valuable information in this way. So I found a runner who was on his own late one night and I asked him to seek information for me."

"I should have given you something to trade," I said. "I never thought of it."

"Indeed, it didn't occur to me either," he said. "I told the boy I acted on behalf of someone who was very senior in Pharaoh's administration and that this person would speak highly of him to Pharaoh himself for helping me."

"That was rather clever of you," Ettu said. "Nobody would think twice about seeing a runner at any hour of the day or night."

"Nor would they pay enough attention to a runner to bother being cautious about what was said in front of him," Merytre added.

"I feel bad at having deceived him in such a way," Half admitted. "He was indeed helpful and it was he who obtained the information I sought. Perhaps if there is a need for me to return again, I could take something for him. My lady might spare him a small gem for his efforts?"

"Of course," I said. "Take whatever you think is appropriate."

So, Half, at least, wasn't considering leaving, despite Amankhau having seen him, although his reasons undoubtedly had more to do with Ettu than me.

"I was hesitant to tell the runner exactly what information I sought," Half continued. "At first, I asked him to listen for anything out of the ordinary. He brought me all sorts of gossip and speculation, some of it interesting, some rather tawdry, but nothing related to what I needed. Piece by piece, I led him closer. First, I told him I sought information about someone who had disappeared, then that it was a woman, then an Ornament. It took him some days after that, but eventually he came to tell me he had heard of a tomb being unsealed secretly to allow an additional body to be added."

"How can you be sure it was my sister?" I asked.

I hardly had time to hope he might be wrong before Half shook his head. Of course, I should have known he would take care to be certain before he brought me such news.

"He described her as a new Ornament from Babylon," he said. "To the best of my knowledge, Princess, you and your sister are the only Babylonian Ornaments."

I might have expected his news to hit me hard. A physical reaction, perhaps a gut-wrenching throb. But all I felt was sadness. Maybe even a little numbness. I certainly didn't feel the way I would have expected on learning the location of my sister's body.

"I am truly regretful to have brought you such sad tidings," Half said. "I know this must cause you great pain."

"This was the news I knew you might bring," I said.

He gave me a solemn nod.

"Will the boy tell anyone about you, do you think?" Ettu asked him.

"I cannot be sure," he admitted. "I don't believe he would volunteer such information. He may tell if asked directly, especially by someone in authority, such as an administrator. But I don't believe he would seek them out."

"It hardly matters now anyway," Sehener said. "Since the boy is there and not here."

I finally realised this was the first time she had encountered Half. She eyed him curiously, but no more than she had done when she first met Tall.

"Has anyone introduced you?" I asked.

"I did," Ettu said quickly.

I tried to see Half from Sehener's eyes. The little man, no more than half the height of a regular man, sat on the edge of the couch, swinging his legs a little as he spoke.

Ettu still clutched his hand and darted fierce looks around the chamber from time to time, as if daring anyone to suggest Half should return to Pharaoh's palace. I doubted she would allow herself to be parted from him again. We had agreed on the ship from Babylon she would leave once my son was born. That would only be another few months, then Ettu would leave, and possibly Half with her, and probably Tall as well. Even Sehener might want to go with them.

Emerging from my thoughts, I realised I had missed whatever Half said next. It seemed to be something about how he obtained food while at Pharaoh's palace. Apparently the runner boy had been useful for more than just information.

"I am glad you weren't hungry," Ettu said to Half.

"I admit there were periods of hunger at first," Half said. "I have never gone without meals before, and there were times I wasn't sure how I would manage, but I always did. It was much easier once the boy started bringing me food."

"What kind of gossip did you hear?" Merytre asked. She

seemed to settle herself more comfortably in her chair and waited with an expectant air.

"Well." Half frowned as he considered her question. "Much of it was about the goings on within Pharaoh's palace. I cannot imagine it would be of interest to you without knowing the actors involved. However, I did hear one thing about folk here which you might find interesting."

Merytre leaned forward, her eyes sparkling.

"Oh, tell us," she said.

"Apparently an Ornament is having an affair with one of the staff," Half said.

I froze. Surely not. If word of my affair had already reached the other palace, it would only be a matter of time before it made its way to Pharaoh himself. How long would it be before somebody figured out who the Ornament was?

"Do you mean Hydna?" Sehener asked.

Half nodded. "With a butler apparently, although I never heard his name. Folk were more interested in the identity of the Ornament than him."

My heart pounded so loudly, it drowned out whatever else Half said. The gossip wasn't about Khaemmalu and me. Not yet anyway.

CHAPTER 20

By the time Half had relayed all his news, and we had caught him up on what happened in his absence, the night was quite late. The kitchen servants brought our evening meal and we ate as we talked. Half, despite his insistence that he had eaten well enough while in hiding, ate much more than usual. Perhaps the food the runner boy supplied him with was sparser than he made out.

As I lay in bed that night, my mind whirled. So many secrets. Ishtar's final location. The two letters to my father. My plan to expose Pharaoh's crimes. Tiye's plan to replace him on the throne. Hydna and Weren. The runner boy who helped Half expecting a reward that would never be paid. Khaemmalu, who I missed with a pang that surprised me with its intensity.

As if he knew I thought about Khaemmalu, my babe suddenly moved. Kick, kick, kick. He doesn't know, the movements seemed to say. The man you love doesn't know about me.

I would have to tell him soon. Very soon. My belly's roundness would be noticeable before long. I had to tell Khaemmalu before he figured it out for himself.

What would he say? I couldn't imagine any man would be

pleased at learning the woman he cared for carried another man's child. Would he be angry? Disappointed? Or would he accept it as something to be expected, given my position as an Ornament? Would he still want me? I had no idea.

As much as I longed to go to Khaemmalu tonight, to tell him about my babe while I had the courage, my eyes kept closing and my limbs felt far too heavy to bother dragging myself out of bed. I fell asleep before I could decide to get up.

I stood in Ishtar's bedchamber, the one she had used here before she was made an Ornament and given her own chambers. She held her hair aside to show me her neck, the evidence of Pharaoh's fingers at her throat already a deepening purple.

Then the bruises faded and she stood in front of me, limp and still, her body broken after Pharaoh's mistreatment.

I woke slowly, the two images lingering in my mind. Ishtar as I had seen her, and Ishtar as I hadn't. Maybe if I kept my eyes open, I could stop myself from seeing the two versions of my sister.

It was early yet, the chamber still dark, with only the faintest tinge of light seeping in around the edges of the shutters. I eventually fell asleep again, and by the time I rose, everyone else was already in the sitting chamber, the kitchen servants had brought our morning meal, and Ettu had sent away my lady's maids.

"It is not like you to sleep so late," she said, sidling up to me as I hesitated at the table where our food was laid out. "Yet this is the second time of late."

"I slept poorly."

I took half a pomegranate and some grainy bread. I had meant to go to the dining chamber this morning, but it was probably too late to catch Henutmire. I hadn't seen her again since she told me Pharaoh had summoned her, but we would have heard by now if she had failed to return. Surely, we would have heard.

"Bad dreams?" Ettu asked. "Or was the babe restless?"

"Something like that," I said and went to sit down.

Since she had made a point of asking privately, I hoped the nearness of the others would mean she wouldn't continue to push me for answers.

Tall and Sehener stood together at a window and seemed to talk quietly, although from what I could see, she was doing most of the speaking. Tall glanced down at her from time to time, his face bemused. He still seemed surprised she was so willing to be near to him. If Sehener noticed his puzzlement, she gave no sign of it.

At first, I had thought them an odd pair, since both were so quiet, but she seemed to talk more to him than to anyone else, and he had managed to start speaking Egyptian in order to communicate with her. Whatever the connection between them, it obviously brought out the best in both.

Merytre let out a peal of laughter at something Half said as a knock came. The men quickly disappeared down the hallway. Had Pharaoh finally decided it was time for me to account for running away from him the other day?

"That will be Ahmose," Merytre said, still chuckling as she headed to the door.

I tried to hide my sigh of relief. I had assumed the old woman was still in bed since she seemed to rise so late these days. Merytre waited until the men were safely hidden away before she opened the door.

The old woman went straight to her chair and collapsed into it. She puffed a little and seemed to have trouble catching her breath. Ettu brought her a mug of beer. I studied Ahmose as she drank, somewhat alarmed at her paleness.

"You must have gone out early," I said once she seemed to breathe more normally.

"Not so early," she answered mildly, peering at me over the top of her mug.

Since she didn't volunteer any information, I didn't ask where she had gone. She might have met with her contact, the one liaising with the librarian for me. Maybe she had even returned with a new spell from him. Perhaps today could be the day I possessed the power I sought. Today might be the day I could begin to put my plan to expose Pharaoh into action.

Exactly how that would happen was still vague to me, although it would involve having enough power to make him fear me. Then I would reveal what he had done without fearing for my own safety, and once everyone knew it, they would surely ensure he was punished for his misdeeds. I couldn't fathom a world in which anyone, even a god, was allowed to do the things Pharaoh had and go unpunished.

The babe kicked, hard, and I winced as I set my hand on my belly.

"You said you weren't unwell," Ettu said.

"I am not," I said. "The babe is kicking."

"May I feel it?" Merytre asked, already getting to her feet in her eagerness.

At my nod, she came to kneel in front of me and placed her hand over my belly. The babe obligingly kicked and her face brightened.

"Oh, my," she said. "It makes him seem very real, doesn't it? I wonder how big he is."

"He must be very small still," I said. "My belly is hardly noticeable yet."

"I cannot wait to meet him," she said. "Only another few months and then..."

Her voice petered away and I pretended I hadn't noticed. I could guess what she avoided saying. My babe would be born in a few months and then he would be taken from me. He would live in Pharaoh's palace and be attended to by wet nurses and all manner of servants. How long would it be before I saw him again? Would they even let me hold him before they took him from me?

Tears welled and I pushed my thoughts away before I started

sobbing. Ahmose had said it was the babe making me feel so emotional and that it might continue until he was born. That knowledge would make me no less embarrassed, though, if I burst into tears in front of everyone.

"I heard something while I was out," Ahmose said, setting her mug aside.

My relief she had distracted everyone from staring at me was short lived when I noticed her solemnity.

"It is about that butler," she said. "Weren."

"The one Half heard about," Merytre said. "He is having an affair with Lady Hydna."

Ahmose gave her a nod. "Remember my sack that was stolen?"

"When you broke your arm?" Ettu asked. "When that horrible man pushed you over and stole your sack with the potion ingredients inside?"

"Apparently it was later found and somehow came into Weren's hands," Ahmose said.

"With your ingredients?" I asked.

Tiye said Weren was looking into whether someone in the Palace was using magic, although I couldn't remember if she had ever said why he thought that was the case. Was Ahmose's sack the reason for his suspicions?

"There must have been something in it," Ahmose said, "because an empty sack wouldn't give him reason for an investigation."

"Surely anyone who found it would see they were herbs and not think twice of it," Merytre said.

"I don't think I have heard about this," Sehener said as she and Tall came to sit with us. "What happened to Ahmose's sack?"

Ettu quickly filled her in on how Ahmose had searched for her when Ettu disappeared while sneaking out to Pharaoh's palace to speak with Tall and Half. A man accosted Ahmose, throwing her to the ground and breaking her arm, then stole the sack containing the potion ingredients she needed to get back in through the gates. It was Khaemmalu who found Ahmose and Ettu and smuggled out more herbs for a new potion to get them in the gates unseen.

"From what I have heard," Ahmose said, "the bottles with the herbs for the potion were still in the sack when it was found. It seems Weren thought they were medical in nature, and only later grew suspicious."

"Because of the odd things that happened?" Ettu asked. "Like the hens that died?"

Ahmose nodded. "Amongst other things. Apparently he decided my sack was evidence of illicit magic use that might be causing such events."

"But he can't have found anything that links your sack to those things," I said. "Nor to you."

Ahmose sank further back into her chair. She seemed breathless now, even though she had done no more than sit and talk.

"Perhaps he knows enough to be suspicious of that combination of herbs," she said. "Or he showed it to someone who does. I don't know. But now he is interviewing anyone who is known to have arcane knowledge."

"Will he want to interview you?" I sat up straighter, alarmed now.

Not that I thought Ahmose would betray us, but I didn't like the thought of someone like Weren getting too close to the truth. If he was clever enough to link Ahmose's sack to magic use, who knew what might trigger his suspicion. It wouldn't take much for the administrators to decide they should search my chambers.

"He might, I suppose," Ahmose admitted. "I have said enough when sourcing herbs that folk know I have some knowledge, even if they think it no more than a healer's ability."

She had said previously she told folk the herbs she sought were for the likes of eye infections and upset bellies. At the time, I had thought her clever to consider such a thing. Of course, we had no reason to anticipate someone like Weren would target those with small amounts of healing knowledge.

"You must tell me at once if Weren calls for you," I said. "I will try to get you out of it."

"Are you sure that would be wise?" Ettu asked. "It may make him wonder what Ahmose has to hide."

Ahmose looked rather pale by now and still breathed too heavily.

"Better that I go and answer his questions," she said. "The sooner he rules me out, the sooner he will turn his attention to someone else."

She leaned her head against the back of the chair and closed her eyes. I wasn't sure whether she signalled she had said all she intended to, or if she was merely exhausted.

"Are you sure we shouldn't fetch a healer?" I asked.

She shook her head just the tiniest bit.

"No, no," she said. "Just let me rest. I find I am rather worn out from so much conversation."

She said nothing further and eventually I assumed she had fallen asleep. Since when had mere conversation been so exhausting for her? When we sailed from Babylon, she would talk for several hours at a time during her lessons.

"This is bad," Ettu said quietly, presumably so as not to disturb Ahmose. "What if Weren wants to interview my lady as well?"

"Then I will answer his questions as best I can," I said.

How many times had I asked Ahmose to show me how to make the potion that got us out of the gates unseen? Yet she had never done so. I stopped asking when she ran out of the special herb for it, since there was no point without that ingredient. Now, I was grateful she had never showed me. Perhaps that was her plan all along — to put me off until I stopped asking, so if she was ever exposed, I would know nothing.

No, it wasn't true I knew nothing. I knew she could make a potion that allowed one to slip unseen past whoever one thought of as they drank it. I had used it myself to leave the grounds the night we went to the House of Life. I also knew about her illicit communication with Messui, who was secretly passing her scrolls taken from Pharaoh's own library.

Unfortunately I wasn't the only one who knew such a thing. Ahmose's contact, whoever she was, knew as much as I did, maybe even more. After all, it was she who communicated with Messui for us. If she was interrogated, she knew enough to implicate both Ahmose and me in a plot to commit heresy. And I didn't even know who she was.

As soon as Ahmose woke, she and I needed to have a very frank discussion.

CHAPTER 21

I passed the time waiting for Ahmose to wake up in worrying. About what she would say if Weren summoned her. What I would say. How much her mystery contact might tell Weren. Whether his investigation would reach as far as Pharaoh's own palace. Would the riches promised to Messui be enough for him to hold his tongue if he was questioned?

When the old woman finally stirred, I went straight to her and took her arm.

"You should lie down," I said, urging her to her feet. "You will be much more comfortable in your bedchamber."

She blinked at me blearily, then shook her head.

"I'm quite fine here," she said.

"Come." I made my voice stern. "I will help you to your chamber."

She didn't argue any further, but let me help her up. She must have guessed I wanted to speak with her in private. Perhaps the others did too, because nobody commented on my sudden desire to help Ahmose to her bedchamber.

I led her to her bed and held her arm to steady her while she lowered herself to sit down.

"Well," she said. "I presume there is something you wish to say."

"I need to know who your contact is," I said. "If you are likely to be summoned, she might be too."

"She will not reveal anything," Ahmose said. "You can trust her."

"How can I know that when I don't even know who she is?"

"You don't need to know." She lay down, then heaved a big sigh. "I must rest. I tire so easily these days."

Although her wan face showed she was indeed fatigued, I suspected she also made a show of it to deter me.

"Ahmose," I said. "I demand you tell me who she is."

"You do not trust me?" she asked. "After everything I have done for you?"

I will be a loyal servant, she had said to me the first time we met. *If you give me reason to be.* At the time, I understood that to mean she saw our relationship as a transaction. I had never had cause to question her loyalty before, but any transaction could be jeopardised if another party offered more. Could Ahmose be bribed? I hated to think such a thing, but she was acting strangely and I couldn't afford to rule out the possibility.

"I must insist," I said.

I swallowed the apology that wanted to come out of my mouth. There was no need to apologise for asking who her contact was. I was her mistress. If I wanted to know such a thing, it was my right. Still, it didn't sit easily with me. I had never treated my companions as servants, or at least, I didn't think I had. They had always been more like friends. Family even. But I needed to know and Ahmose wouldn't tell me unless I pushed her.

"Her name is Henuttawy," she said at last.

Tiye had a maid by that name. The way Ahmose held my gaze suggested she waited for me to understand.

"Tiye's maid?" No wonder Tiye had hinted at suspecting I knew something about the illicit magic use Weren was convinced had occurred. Her maid had probably reported her interactions with Ahmose to her.

"She is my daughter," Ahmose said.

Stunned, I could only blink at her for a few moments. I had never paid much attention to Henuttawy's face. If she looked like her mother, I hadn't noticed.

"Tiye's maid," I said again, wondering whether I had misunderstood. Henuttawy could be a common name. There might be any number of women in the Palace with that name.

Ahmose nodded, a small smile playing over her lips.

I knew she had a daughter, of course. On the journey from Babylon, Ahmose told me that when she was given to one of her dead husband's creditors, she was also parted from her daughter. My mind whirled and I hardly knew what to say.

"Why didn't you tell us?" I asked.

"At first, I merely wanted to keep it to myself for a little while," she said. "But then as the days passed, I didn't know how. Eventually, it became a secret I had kept for too long to share."

"You must have known it would come out eventually," I said.

"Perhaps."

"How did you find out?"

As my thoughts clarified, I found I had so many questions, I hardly knew where to start. Did Tiye know about Henuttawy's relationship with Ahmose? How much did Henuttawy know about the secrets we kept in my chambers? What had she told Tiye? Why didn't Tiye tell me she knew?

Tiye was a formidable woman and I couldn't imagine one of her maids successfully keeping such a secret from her. If she hadn't told me, it was because she planned to use that information at some point. Tiye always had a reason for what she did, even if I couldn't figure out what it was at the time. I finally realised Ahmose hadn't answered me. I shook her arm.

"Ahmose," I said. This was no time for her to fall asleep again. I needed answers.

She roused and opened her eyes with a sigh. I would have felt bad about disturbing her if the secret she had been hiding wasn't so dangerous.

"How long have you known?" I asked.

"Since a day or two after we arrived," she admitted. "Henuttawy sought me out because she had heard of the arrival of some Babylonians. She never knew the name of the man I was given to, but she did hear some time later that a man who had come into possession of a servant woman in payment of her husband's debts had gone to Babylon. She never knew whether that was me, but when she heard of some arrivals from Babylon, she came to ask if I might know of her mother."

"How did you establish she was your daughter?"

Could Ahmose be wrong? Surely after being parted for so long, neither mother nor daughter would recognise each other. Ahmose had said she lived in Babylon for at least thirty years. That meant Henuttawy must be in her mid thirties. I hadn't realised she was so old. She would have been too young to remember her mother and surely Ahmose wouldn't recognise her babe as a grown woman. But Ahmose gave me a look that suggested I couldn't possibly understand.

"A mother always knows," she said. "I recognised her from the moment I saw her."

"Did she know you?" I asked.

"She thought it might be me, but didn't know how to ask. She was only four years old when she was taken from me, but she somehow held onto the memory of my face. I didn't tell her at first because, frankly, I was too surprised. I never imagined we might be reunited, let alone it might be she who found me. It was inconceivable that after all these years apart, and so much distance between us, we would find each other again."

"And Tiye," I said. "Does she know?"

Ahmose hesitated.

"The truth, please," I said.

"Yes," she admitted, closing her eyes again. "Lady Tiye knows Henuttawy is my daughter."

How many times had I been in Tiye's chambers while Henuttawy was there? How many times had Tiye amused herself in thinking about the connection between her maid and my companion, and never bothered to tell me? She likely had a plan to reveal it, but it would be at a time that benefitted herself.

Fury welled within me. They had both been lying to me all this time. I was hardly surprised at Tiye. Despite our alliance, I knew she still played her own game. But Ahmose's betrayal disappointed me. I expected more from her.

I left her bedchamber before I said something hasty I would regret later.

CHAPTER 22

"I am going to visit Tiye," I announced as I strode through the sitting chamber.

"Now?" Ettu asked. "She won't expect you so late in the day."

"Now." I waited at the door, giving Tall and Half time to leave before I unbarred it.

"I will go with you," Merytre said quickly.

Ettu didn't argue and Merytre followed me out. In truth, I was pleased it was her and not Ettu. She would be less likely to interrogate me.

At Tiye's chambers, I raised my hand to knock, but hesitated. What if Henuttawy answered the door? My fury was no doubt obvious and she would immediately realise I knew who she was. But it was Bennerib who answered.

"Kassaya." Tiye was arranged on a couch, looking as if she waited for a visitor. But then, perhaps she was. Just because I typically only visited her in the morning didn't mean others did the same.

If she wondered at my arrival so close to sunset, she made no comment, only gestured towards the facing couch. I sat and smoothed my skirt over my knees to give me a few moments to think. Already I regretted my hasty decision to come straight here. I should have waited until I felt calmer and knew what I wanted to say.

I met Tiye's gaze and she arched her eyebrows at me, an indication she knew I had come for a particular reason.

"Where is Henuttawy?" I asked.

Tiye was an expert at controlling her face, but I didn't miss how she glanced away for the briefest moment, before she gave me a cool stare.

"She has gone to deliver a message for me," she said.

I thought she might offer some detail since it must be clear I knew. There was no other reason for me to ask after her maid. But she only looked at me and waited.

"Why didn't you tell me?" The words burst out before I could decide how best to frame them.

She gave me a questioning look, which only served to infuriate me even more. She knew exactly what I referred to, but she would make me say it. I should have expected it.

"You knew Ahmose was your maid's mother," I said.

"Aah." Tiye leaned back against the couch, her face thoughtful, as if this was new information.

I clenched my jaw and tried to stop myself from saying anything more. She owed me an explanation and the only way I would get it from her was with my silence.

"It was not my news to share," she said with a shrug that suggested the matter was of little importance to her.

"That doesn't normally bother you." I was well aware of how bitter I sounded and her raised eyebrow showed she didn't miss it either. "How long have you known?"

She made a show of pondering my question.

"Since shortly after your arrival," she said. "If I recall correctly, Henuttawy told me the day after she found out."

All this time, she had known. How many hours had I spent sitting here in her chambers while she kept this secret to herself?

"It appears to be a problem for you," she observed. "That I knew and you didn't."

I inhaled sharply, and tried to think before I spoke. Why indeed was it such a problem? Both Ahmose and Tiye had lied to me, even if by their silence rather than their words. But other than my hurt feelings, was any damage done? It was a good thing for Ahmose to be reunited with the daughter she was separated from for so many years. But if they kept this one secret from you, a bitter voice inside me whispered, what else are they hiding?

"It shows I cannot trust you." I looked Tiye right in the eyes as I spoke, daring her to contradict me. I should have known she wouldn't.

"Surely you have been here long enough to know you can't trust anybody in this place?" Her tone was cool, making it clear she thought nothing of my accusation.

"I thought we were friends. That we were in alliance."

"In alliance, yes." Still her gaze was cool and untroubled. "Friends, though? A wise woman will not seek friendship here. What have I ever done that would suggest we were friends?"

"I offered you friendship," I said. "In exchange for not cleaning your bathing chamber. I have visited you many times. Sat and conversed with you. Shared information with you."

Shared my feelings, even. I had shown vulnerability in front of Tiye, something I now realised may have been a mistake.

"And how many times have I visited you in return?" she asked.

The realisation hit me hard. Tiye had accepted my friendship, but she never returned it. Why hadn't I ever wondered why she never came to visit me? She sat here in her chambers and expected others to pay court to her, as if she was a queen. But she wasn't. She was only an Ornament and no better than me. I, at least, was a princess. She couldn't claim the same. I got to my feet.

"I must be going," I said. "I don't expect I shall visit you again."

Tiye said nothing as I crossed the chamber. Bennerib opened the door and silently closed it behind me.

At the end of Tiye's hallway, Merytre waited, now joined by Ettu. They didn't need to tell me they had been discussing Ahmose's revelation. Their faces made it obvious. Ahmose must have told them after I left, and Ettu came rushing to tell Merytre.

Irritation prickled within me. Ettu just couldn't wait to share the gossip, could she? What else had they talked about while I was gone? What other secrets were kept within my chambers without my knowledge? I strode past them without speaking and turned down the hallway that led away from my chambers.

"My lady?" came Ettu's voice as they hurried after me. "Do you intend to go for a walk?"

"I shall do as I please and it is not your place to question me," I snapped.

I immediately regretted my reckless words, although Ettu's clearing of her throat — a pointed comment on my rudeness — only irritated me even more.

"You may return to my chambers," I said over my shoulder. "I do not require your company at present."

"But—" Ettu started.

"Go," I said.

I didn't look back and never slowed my pace, but I no longer heard them behind me. If they wanted to gossip like servants, that's how I would treat them. I had been too good to them, letting them live in my chambers instead of the maids' dormitories, eating the food provided for me, and becoming something that was almost family.

My feet slowed as I started down the stairs and already I regretted my rudeness. Given it must be dusk by now, Ettu might have come to walk me back so Merytre could go home. Sutem would have finished his shift and no doubt waited for her. He always waited so she didn't walk home alone after dark. The women had probably just paused to chat for a few moments, then I returned and was horribly rude to them.

Halfway down the stairs, I stopped. I should go back and apologise. Even though we didn't believe the danger lay in this palace, we still tried to ensure none of us went out alone. If I went back now, Ettu and I could see Merytre to Sutem and then continue on for a walk.

I turned and even went back up a couple of steps before changing my mind. As I reached the ground floor, I realised my mistake in continuing alone.

At the main entrance stood Amankhau talking to a man I didn't recognise. He was a little taller than Amankhau and his bare chest displayed muscles which were more clearly defined than those of the administrator. Another of the modified men, of course. He wouldn't be permitted within the Palace walls otherwise.

To leave through the front doors, I would have to walk right past them. Alone. It was either that, or scurry back up the stairs. Amankhau could hardly miss seeing me if I left, and he would know it was because I wanted to avoid him.

The last time I had spoken to him was the day Half returned and I convinced Amankhau he imagined seeing an unknown person with me. I could hardly hope he had forgotten, but I prayed he wouldn't mention it. Hopefully, he was embarrassed at how I thought he was suffering from the heat and needed a healer.

Taking a deep breath, I crossed the chamber. I fixed my gaze on the doors and tried to pretend I didn't see Amankhau. *Please Marduk, let me make it past him without having to speak to him just this once.* But Marduk wasn't listening, or perhaps he disagreed about the benefit of me avoiding Amankhau.

"Lady Kassaya." Amankhau's voice was as oily as ever.

I barely glanced at him as I hurried past, trying to give the impression I had somewhere else to be.

"Administrator." My tone was curt and I kept moving. I almost made it past them before he spoke again.

"I don't believe you have met Weren yet," he said.

My feet slowed. Of course, he wouldn't let me make a swift escape. A heartbeat or two passed, before I realised what he had said. Weren. The butler having an affair with Hydna and who was also investigating the use of magic. The one who had Ahmose's sack. I couldn't walk away now. It might make Weren even more suspicious if he thought I tried to avoid speaking with him. I turned back to them.

"No, I haven't." I rearranged my face in what I hoped was a polite expression as I nodded at Weren.

He bowed and seemed to take his time eyeing me up and down. I searched for some sign of what made him so appealing to Hydna that she was willing to disregard the rules. He was pleasant enough to look at, but nothing exceptional. Not like Khaemmalu.

"Well met, my lady," Weren said. "We were just discussing you, as a matter of fact."

"Oh?" I kept my tone cool and hoped they didn't realise how my heart suddenly pounded.

"Yes, Weren was telling me a rather interesting story about finding a sack full of, ah, *herbal* items," Amankhau said, his heavy emphasis on herbal indicating he meant something more. "Apparently he has traced it back to one of your servants. An old woman by the name of Ahmose, I believe."

"That would be my tutor," I said. "She can be useful when any of us are unwell. Her knowledge of herbs has helped to calm upset bellies and eased the pain of small injuries like bruises."

I hoped my nonchalance would assure them there was no reason to look any more closely at Ahmose, but the men exchanged glances.

"Weren will need to interview her," Amankhau said. "To

determine exactly what knowledge she has and how it has been used."

"I just told you," I said, letting myself sound irritated. "She does not have the same level of knowledge as a healer, but she is useful on occasion."

"Weren will be best placed to determine the extent of her knowledge," Amankhau said. "He will send a runner when he is ready to interview her."

"And you as well, of course, my lady," Weren said. He, at least, made a show of sounding civil. "I need to establish what you know about her actions."

"Her actions?" I asked.

He waved away the question.

"Your interview will be soon enough to discuss that," he said. "Now, if you will excuse me, I have some messages to send."

CHAPTER 23

Weren left and I took the opportunity to depart at the same time, not wanting to risk any moment in which I found myself alone with Amankhau. Outside, the sun was in the midst of setting, casting the sky in a glorious shade of orange. It wasn't quite as late as I had thought.

I headed along the path where Khaemmalu and I usually met, although it was probably too early for him to be on duty yet. No matter, I would take a long walk, and by the time I circled back, he would surely be here.

As I walked, my mind filled with Khaemmalu's face, the feel of his lips on mine and his hands on my body. I caught my sandal on the path and stumbled, the shock of it tearing me from my thoughts. I slowed my pace and tried to be more mindful of where I placed my feet.

I walked until the sun finished setting and darkness shrouded the grounds. I neither saw nor heard any sign of Khaemmalu, or any other guard for that matter, although from time to time, I felt like somebody was nearby. I paused beneath an acacia tree to lean against its trunk. I had walked quite a long way and my feet were sore. If I rested here for a while, perhaps Khaemmalu would find me on my way back.

The feeling that someone watched me came again. Trying to look casual, I scanned my surroundings. It was probably a guard, or maybe even the seer. She watched me from the shadows one time and only came out when I demanded she show herself. But although I still felt someone nearby, I saw no sign of whoever it was. It was like that moment in my bedchamber, when I had been certain someone was there.

As I pushed myself off the trunk, ready to resume my walk, the scent of frankincense came again. I froze, one hand still on the bark, noting absently its roughness beneath my fingers.

The gardens were full of flowers and it was a rare night that the air wasn't filled with their perfume, but they never smelled like this. Perhaps a new flower bloomed. Something I hadn't encountered before and which smelled enough like frankincense to be mistaken for it.

The scent grew stronger until if I had been standing there with my eyes closed, I would have thought somebody wearing the perfume was right beside me. But despite the darkness, I could make out enough to see I was alone.

"Ishtar?" I asked softly, grateful there was nobody to hear such foolishness from me.

She wasn't buried with the correct rites, so maybe she had left the afterlife, come back to the mortal world in search of sunshine and company. I could think of no other explanation for why I kept smelling my sister's perfume.

I set off again, more slowly this time since my feet were sore from such a long walk. The scent of frankincense drifted with me for a few moments, and then, as suddenly as it had come, the aroma was gone.

Khaemmalu didn't reveal himself until just as I reached the last of the shadowy places where we could be hidden from spying eyes.

"Kassaya." His voice was soft, pitched for my ears only.

I followed him into the shadows. His hand found mine and I clung to him, marvelling in the warmth of his fingers, the simple joy of being connected with another human in this physical way.

"Back here," he said.

He led me deep into the shrubbery. The place where he finally stopped looked no different to any of the other shadowy spots we snuck through, but he seemed to know this was where he had intended to take me. He stopped and turned to pull me against his chest. He murmured into my hair, something I didn't catch.

"What was that?" I asked, barely able to speak with my face pressed to his chest. His wonderful, warm, firm chest. I breathed deeply, filling my lungs with the scent that was somehow all his own.

He moved back a little, just enough to speak.

"Have you received any messages from Pharaoh?" he asked.

I stilled in his arms. With the distraction of Half's return, I had almost forgotten Pharaoh's anger.

"No," I said. "Should I have?"

He made a noise, something between a sigh and a groan.

"He was furious after your game," he said. "Bebi told me—"

He stopped abruptly, as if realising he had been about to say something he didn't want to.

"Bebi told you what?" I searched his face, although I could see little other than a shadow.

"It is nothing," he said.

His hand on the back of my head pulled me against his chest again and his lips nuzzled my ear. I moved away from his mouth, only because I couldn't think while he was doing that, not because I wanted him to stop.

"Khaemmalu, tell me what Bebi said."

He sighed and gave up on nibbling my ear.

"Pharaoh was angry after you left the other night," he said.

It was no more than he had already told me.

"Go on," I urged.

He sighed again.

"Khaemmalu."

I pulled away from him, although my body instantly craved his. I wanted to lean against him again. To bury my face in his chest. To let his hands do unspeakably wonderful things to my body. I made myself stay there, just out of his reach.

"He took his anger out on one of the servants." His tone was brusque now. "And that is all I intend to tell you, so there is no point in continuing to ask."

My heart ached with sudden intensity.

"A female servant?" I wanted to be sure I hadn't misunderstood. I knew I hadn't, but I needed to hear him say it.

Khaemmalu sighed. "Yes."

"Is she…" I didn't know how to say it. Please Marduk, let it not be that a woman lost her life because he was angry with me.

"Oh, no," he said, as if only now realising what I must have thought. "She is alive, but injured. Bebi said she has not returned to the palace since that night."

"Is he sure…"

"He went to her home to check on her. He saw her with his own eyes."

My legs went weak with relief and I swayed forward. Khaemmalu caught me and pulled me back against him.

"I thought…" My voice was muffled against his chest and I stopped, realising I didn't need to say it. He already knew what I thought.

"I thanked Amun you got out of there," he confessed, his lips once again working at my ear. "I don't think I could bear it if…"

"I know, but Khaemmalu, I will have to go back. When he summons me next."

His mouth stilled, although his breath was still hot against my ear.

"You should leave," he said. "Go while you can."

"Go where?"

"Anywhere. I will go with you."

For a few moments, I let myself imagine it. The two of us, on a ship, sailing off to… My thoughts ground to a halt. I couldn't leave.

How could I walk away knowing it would break the alliance between Babylon and Egypt? If Pharaoh took his armies to Babylon, how many people would die because of me? How many women would become widows, how many children would be fatherless, and all because I refused to do what my father asked of me? The only thing he had ever asked.

"I cannot," I said. "I am the seal on the alliance. I wish you would stop asking."

I felt, rather than heard, his sigh against my hair.

"I know," he said.

CHAPTER 24

I left Khaemmalu reluctantly and only because my belly growled so loudly, he heard it and led me back to the path. We stopped in the last of the shadows, where he kissed me one final time. Just before I left, he bent to pick up something, then pressed it into my hand. A flower, by the feel of it.

"Good night," he whispered, then gave me a little shove towards the path.

I tried to act casual in case anyone watched me. As I reached the torch-lit path, I looked at the thing Khaemmalu had given me. A narcissus, its yellow petals open like a mouth. It couldn't be a coincidence. It was part of the message. Another piece in the puzzle that someone was leading me to unravel.

As I approached the main entrance, I spotted Ettu. She stood not far from the guards, close enough to be secure in their nearness, but far enough that it was clear she wasn't conversing with them. She studied me as I approached.

"A pleasant walk, my lady?" Her voice was cool, the hurt plain.

"Yes, thank you. Why are you here?"

"I walked Merytre out and thought to wait for you. To walk you back, of course."

I had wondered when I saw her there whether she had something she wanted to say privately, but it seemed she was just doing her job of ensuring I was not left alone. Tears burned and I hurried inside, not wanting her to spot them.

It was stupid of me, really. I had been sterner than she deserved and I had treated her like a servant. If she now treated me as nothing more than her mistress, it was no more than I deserved. We made our way back up the stairs in silence. It was only as we turned down the last hallway that I found the courage to say what I knew I should.

"I'm sorry," I said. "I was wrong to treat you like that."

She gave me a stiff nod, although I felt her tension ease.

"A runner came while you were out," she said. "With a message from Weren."

"I met him earlier," I said. "He was talking with Amankhau."

"He has called Ahmose for an interview tomorrow."

My feet slowed as we approached my door.

"I didn't expect it to be so soon." Even though we were alone in the hallway, I kept my voice low. "Will I be permitted to go with her, do you think?"

"The runner said Ahmose was to attend Weren alone. I'm sure she can handle it. You know she is very capable."

And I would probably do no more than make a mess of it if I went with her anyway. I would say the wrong thing and give Weren even more reason to be suspicious.

"What if they want to search my chambers?" I whispered.

"That was my fear too," she said. "Perhaps they should leave tonight."

"But where would they go? They cannot return to Pharaoh's palace."

They were too conspicuous, given their unique appearances, and Userhet would try again to kill Half, and there would be too many questions about where they had been and why they had suddenly returned. Their reappearance would probably draw even more attention than their disappearance.

"Perhaps they could go to Sutem's house?" Ettu suggested. "I am sure he would take them in. Merytre could take food home with her each day, so it would be no burden on Sutem to provide for them."

"But they would have to stay inside and away from the windows," I said. "They could never let anyone see them. It would be no better for them than being here."

Worse, perhaps, because they would no doubt be confined to a much smaller area. I had never seen Sutem's house and had no idea how big it was, but it must surely be smaller than my chambers. And depending on how close his neighbours were, Tall and Half would have to be very careful nobody heard them. At least here, they could speak reasonably freely without worrying about being heard.

"Maybe it would only need to be for a day or two," Ettu said. "Just until Weren has interviewed Ahmose and decided she doesn't know anything. Then they could come back."

"But she doesn't have any of the special herb for her potion," I said. "And she would need enough to make two doses for each of them."

A dose each to get them out of the gates and another to get back in. I didn't know how much of the herb she needed, but four doses would surely take too much, considering she had none at present.

"I don't know," I said. "Let's see what Ahmose thinks."

But when we reached my chambers, Ahmose had already gone to bed.

"Did she eat first?" Ettu asked, as she surveyed the food the kitchen maids had laid out for us.

She offered me a plate, but I shook my head and she handed it to Tall instead. My stomach was still all fluttery after being with Khaemmalu. I couldn't eat yet.

"She had already gone to bed before the food was delivered," Sehener said. "I was a bit worried, to be honest. She looked very pale."

"She didn't have breakfast either," Ettu said.

Now I thought about it, I couldn't remember the last time I saw Ahmose eat.

"She must be worried about her interview," Sehener suggested. "I know I would be."

"She didn't know about that before breakfast," Ettu said.

But Ahmose did already know there was reason to think Weren might summon her. Perhaps that was why she had looked so pale lately. She must be very worried about how close Weren was to uncovering our secrets.

"Oh, did you pick a flower?" Sehener asked. "Let me put it in some water for you."

I had forgotten the narcissus still clutched in my hand. Even though they surely knew there was something between Khaemmalu and me, I was reluctant to admit it was from him.

"I saw it on my way back," I said.

Ettu gave me an odd look, as if she knew I lied. I pretended not to notice and busied myself with some baked fish even though I didn't want it.

Sehener set a mug containing the narcissus on a table and gave me a pleased smile. I nodded a thank you at her.

Ettu and Sehener tried to keep a conversation going, but it soon petered out and they fell silent. I had mostly been tuning them out anyway, preferring instead to worry about Ahmose's upcoming interview with Weren. I went to bed early, although I lay sleepless for a long time.

When the bird outside my window began its dawn song, I woke with my head fuzzy from such a late night. It seemed like far too much bother to get out of bed, but Ettu would probably come to see if I was ill if I didn't. She had already commented on how late I was rising recently.

Out in the sitting chamber, Ettu and Half sat together, their heads close as they talked. They pulled a little apart when they saw me, and Ettu gave me an embarrassed smile. I pretended I hadn't noticed and poured myself some beer.

A knock came at the door and they both jumped up, Half to hurry back to the men's bedchamber and Ettu to let Merytre in. I breathed a sigh of relief that it was only Merytre and not a messenger from Pharaoh.

Merytre beamed and looked like she had slept far better than I had. I pushed away my irritation and tried to hide my crankiness. It wasn't her fault I had slept poorly.

My maids soon arrived and the daily ritual of being stripped naked began. Sitting on the stool in my bathing chamber, I closed my eyes and tried to pretend I was somewhere else. It didn't matter where, only that wherever it was, I wore clothes. And as long as my eyes were closed, I didn't have to see Abar glaring at me. I wished I could at least tell her I had tried to find a way for her to see her sister's body, but it would only make things worse. She would say I hadn't tried hard enough.

My thoughts drifted. Khaemmalu. Ahmose's search for scrolls of power. Tiye's plan to replace Pharaoh on the throne. My sister. Half's news that Hydna and Weren's affair was the subject of gossip in Pharaoh's palace. It was the scent of frankincense that drew me from my thoughts. The same earthy scent I had been smelling of late.

"Who is wearing frankincense?" I asked.

Khensa, who knelt in front of me as she massaged lotion into my feet, glanced up at me briefly, but shook her head. Someone just out of my line of sight murmured, "not me, my lady", followed by someone else's "nor I".

One of the women was busy arranging my wig and I couldn't move my head. Khensa was the only one I could see properly, positioned as I was, and she had already returned to her task.

"Is nobody wearing that scent?" I asked.

"Frankincense is not for the likes of us, my lady," someone said. Tuya, I thought, from her voice. "It is far too expensive."

"I have never worn frankincense in my life," someone else said.

"I don't imagine I ever shall," another said. "Not unless I marry a very rich man."

A giggle from another woman.

"But can't you smell it?" I asked. "Someone in here is wearing it."

The hands on me stilled as they all sniffed the air.

"I don't smell it, my lady," Khensa said.

"Am I the only one who does?" I asked.

Silence greeted my question.

"Perhaps it is something that smells somewhat like frankincense," Sehener said at last. "That is probably why we are all confused."

"Then who is wearing a scent that is similar to it?" I asked.

More silence and they all seemed to very carefully avoid looking at me.

I gave up. I didn't think I was imagining it, but perhaps I was so desperate to resolve things with my sister that I fooled myself into thinking she lingered here. Knowing she had been interred without the correct rites only encouraged such thoughts.

As the women moved around me, filing my nails, applying lotion, making up my face, and the many other daily grooming tasks that seemed completely unnecessary, I again caught sight of Abar. She stood in her usual place by the door, and as always, she held herself tall with her head high.

Seeing her stand like that made me wonder, and not for the first time, what her life had been like in Nubia. She never acted like she considered herself to be a servant and she certainly didn't stand like one. The difference now was this new, grim way she glared at me. As if she hated me. Normally she acted as if she couldn't see any of us.

Her fierceness made me want to placate her. To please her. The way I used to want to please Ishtar because she was so perfect and elegant, and I knew I could never measure up to her.

At last, my maids finished my ablutions and filed out, each of them wishing me a cheery good day as she left, all except Abar who, as usual, was the first out the door and said not a word of farewell.

CHAPTER 25

My stomach growled loudly as the door closed behind the maids. The sickness I had suffered during those first weeks after my babe was conceived had definitely passed and now I seemed to be hungry all the time. The kitchen servants had brought our morning meal and my mouth watered at the aroma of freshly-baked bread and warm gruel. My longing to stop and eat right now warred with the need to check on Henutmire.

Ahmose sat with a bowl balanced on her lap, but she didn't seem to be eating. Her face was still pale today, although perhaps not as bad as last night.

"Are you nervous about your interview?" Ettu asked her, sitting down beside Tall.

Ahmose seemed to consider her words carefully before she replied.

"Nervous, no," she said. "I admit, however, I am somewhat concerned about what Weren knows, or thinks he knows."

"Have you thought about how you will answer his questions?" Ettu asked.

"I will tell him only as much as would be reasonable for a

woman with some small amount of herbal knowledge," Ahmose said. "Anything past that, I shall pretend not to understand."

"I wish I could get you out of the interview," I said.

"You need not worry for me, Princess," she replied. "I know how to look after myself."

Indeed, she had killed the man she was given to after her husband died. He had been cruel to her, from what I understood, and she seemed to feel no guilt. When I first learned of it, I hadn't understood how a woman might want to escape so badly that she would kill someone. Even now, I probably didn't fully understand, but I certainly had some comprehension.

Sehener offered to accompany me to the dining chamber, although I didn't miss the way she eyed our meal. Although I said I could wait while she ate, she insisted she wasn't hungry yet.

But when we reached the dining chamber, Henutmire wasn't there. It was a rare day she didn't eat here and I lingered over my meal, hoping she might arrive late, but she never came.

I puzzled over Henutmire's absence as Sehener and I headed back to my chambers, and I caught her giving me a few glances before she finally spoke.

"Does something trouble you, my lady?" she asked.

"I was hoping to speak with Henutmire," I said. "She wasn't there today."

"Perhaps you could visit her in her chambers," Sehener offered, her voice bright with this opportunity to be helpful. "If she is feeling poorly, she would likely welcome a visit from a friend."

I wasn't sure Henutmire would call me a friend, but it wouldn't be the first time I had visited her and she would surely appreciate my concern. But when we reached Henutmire's chambers, nobody answered her door, despite Sehener knocking several times.

"I can come back later and ask when it would be convenient for you to visit her?" she offered.

I fretted over Henutmire's absence all the way back to my chambers. But if she hadn't returned from Pharaoh's palace, surely word would already have gone out, and her maids would not have been reassigned so soon. Somebody would be there in her chambers, waiting for their mistress's return, and they would answer a knock at the door.

Sehener and I had only just sat down before a runner boy arrived to take Ahmose to Weren. The men slipped away, but not without pausing for Half to whisper something to Ahmose and for Tall to give her an awkward pat on the shoulder. Ahmose groaned with the effort of rising from her chair and her face had gone quite pale again.

"Perhaps one of us should come with you," I said.

"No, no," she replied with a wave of her hand as she made her slow way to the door. "The runner yesterday said I was to come alone. It wouldn't do to aggravate Weren before my interview even starts."

I saw the sense in that and didn't push any further, even though I had only meant one of us should walk with her.

"I'm sure she will be fine," Ettu said after Ahmose left, although she didn't sound convinced. "She is a sensible woman and will not say anything to arouse suspicion."

But Ahmose didn't know how much Weren knew. She might say the wrong thing without realising. Ettu gave me a hard look, as if she suspected I disagreed, and wondered why I said nothing. Not wanting to argue with her, I pretended not to notice.

Another knock came just as Tall and Half returned to the sitting chamber. They froze and we all turned towards the door, as if we somehow thought whoever it was would see right through the wood and spy them standing there.

"That didn't sound like Ahmose," Merytre whispered.

I had feared a messenger from Pharaoh, come to summon me to account for running away from him. I hadn't even thought it might be Ahmose already.

Ettu cleared her throat.

"Who is it?" she called.

"Iyroy," came an officious male voice. "Pharaoh's personal physician. I have been sent to examine the Lady Kassaya."

Ettu waved Tall and Half away, but they were already tiptoeing back to their bedchamber. She followed to lock their door. I leaned back against the couch and smoothed my skirt over my knees, trying to look at ease. I should have expected this. Really, it was surprising the physician hadn't come earlier. Pharaoh would, of course, want to make sure everything was progressing well with his son.

When Merytre let the physician in, I was surprised to see he was older than I expected, maybe even as old as thirty. He wore a pleated linen robe that came down to his sandals and a chin-length wig. His belly poked out a little beneath the robe. Clearly, this was a man who ate well. He scanned the chamber, then focussed in on me.

"Perhaps you would prefer this examination to occur in the privacy of your bedchamber?" he asked, surprising me with his thoughtfulness.

I couldn't risk taking him to my bedchamber. If he looked a little further down the hallway, he might spot the door with the lock on it. And he might mention to Panouk or Amankhau that I had a locked door, and they would surely know there used to be no lock there.

"Here will be quite fine," I said.

Ettu, Merytre and Sehener went to stand at the window with their backs to me, which I supposed was their way of giving me some privacy. Although I appreciated the gesture, I wished someone had stayed with me. The way Iyroy eyed me was making me feel quite apprehensive.

"Well, then," he said. "Perhaps you would care to lie down?"

I swivelled around to put my feet up on the couch. To my relief, Ettu came to place a cushion under my head and straighten my skirt. As the physician dropped to his knees beside me, my heart felt like it pounded in my ears. I had no idea what such an examination might involve.

"Stay," I said to Ettu as she went to leave again. "Please."

She nodded and came back to stand behind the couch, although she turned to face a little off to the side. I guessed she had more of an idea than I did of what was about to happen.

Iyroy put his hands on my belly and probed it. It was much the same as what Ahmose did when I fell ill after dining with Pharaoh and the familiarity relaxed me somewhat. This was nothing unbearable.

Ishtar was ill then too and she lost her babe. The memory of our awkward final conversation brought tears to my eyes.

"Does that hurt?" Iyroy asked.

"No," I said.

He grunted a little and I was thankful he didn't ask why I cried if he wasn't hurting me. He poked at me a little longer, than cleared his throat.

"I need to do an internal examination now," he said.

"A... what?"

He gestured towards my legs. "Perhaps your lady's maid would hold up your skirt?"

My face must have shown my panic, because he waved away Ettu who already had my hem in her hands.

"We shall leave that for next time," he said. "When you are more prepared for such an examination."

I only nodded, too overwhelmed to speak. My emotions were a mix of mortification that Iyroy intended to look under my skirt, and embarrassment that he might even put his hands there, and a completely irrational desire to burst into laughter, along with sorrow at the memory of that last terse conversation with Ishtar.

Iyroy bowed and let himself out. Ettu followed him to bar the door, and while she was busy, I sat up and rearranged my skirt.

"Well, that wasn't so bad, was it?" She gave me an overly bright smile.

"It wasn't your belly he was poking," I said grumpily, even though I agreed with her.

"Perhaps next time you might allow him to inspect you in your bedchamber, though," she said. "For privacy. Tall and Half will just have to be very still and silent."

"I thought it was too dangerous to go down there," I said. "He might see the lock."

"Hmm," she said. "Maybe we can hide it. Stack some chests or something in front of the door and tell him we are rearranging some of the chambers."

"That is not a bad idea," Sehener said, coming to sit down. "Although I don't know how we will explain it when the rearranging continues through every visit he makes."

Merytre returned with Tall and Half behind her, and they too took their usual places.

"I imagine such a visit from the royal physician might be a frequent event from now on, Princess?" Half asked, somewhat delicately.

"I suppose," I said.

I should have asked when he would come again. It would be nice to know how long I had to prepare myself for the next examination.

Tall gestured, a funny movement with his hand, which I couldn't interpret.

"Oh, yes," Sehener said. "A screen, my lady. We could set up a screen out here, so you can be examined in privacy without having to take the physician to your bedchamber."

"That is a good idea," I said. "Where would we get one from?"

"Make!" Tall said. "Me!"

He mimed a hammering action.

"I can help you with that, buddy," Half said. "As long as the screen isn't too high."

Ettu snorted at his self-deprecating comment, but I only blinked at Half. It was the first time I had ever heard him joke about his height and I didn't quite know how to react. It felt wrong to laugh at him. Ettu obviously didn't think so, though, and maybe I should take her lead, but I had spent too long agonising about it and it was too late to laugh now.

"Wood!" Tall said. "Nails!" He frowned and seemed to search for the word he wanted. "Hammer!"

"And some linen to fasten over it," Merytre added. "Tall, if there is anything else you need, tell me before I leave tonight. Sutem will be able to get the wood and the tools for you."

"Do we need to worry about the noise?" Ettu asked, but Merytre waved her question away.

"I cannot tell you how many times I have heard hammering or banging or some such sound as I have walked through the Palace," she said. "Some of the Ornaments seem to redecorate their chambers every few weeks. There is a whole team of workmen available to do such things. Modified men, of course."

She seemed to carefully avoid looking at either Tall or Half, as if embarrassed at mentioning such a thing in front of them.

"I would think the risk of anyone happening to pass by at the wrong time is quite minimal," Half said. "As I understand it, this hallway leads only here and to Lady Tiye's chambers."

Ettu confirmed this with a nod.

"I can fetch some linen from the sewers," Sehener offered. "Would you want any particular colour, my lady?"

"Oh, no," I said. "Anything will do."

It seemed like a waste of perfectly good fabric, but I did like the idea of a privacy screen. If Iyroy's visits were to be a regular thing, a screen would make his examinations that tiny bit more bearable for me, without endangering Tall and Half any more than necessary.

CHAPTER 26

When the next knock came, we all expected it to be Ahmose, but Merytre shook her head.

"That doesn't sound like her either," she said.

As usual, Ettu waited until the men were safely locked away before she answered the door.

"Oh," she said, flinging the door wide open.

Weren and Panouk came in carrying Ahmose between them. As they lay her on the couch where Half and Ettu usually sat, Panouk used his foot to push away the little stool Half used to climb up. I held my breath, waiting for him to ask about it, but he said nothing, and eventually I realised he probably assumed someone rested their feet on it.

Ahmose seemed dazed, her eyelids fluttering as she turned her head from side to side. She tried to say something, but all that came out was an unintelligible groan.

"What happened?" I didn't know whether to direct my question towards Weren or Panouk.

"She collapsed while I was interviewing her," Weren said. "She did already look rather pale when she arrived. I assumed she was

141

nervous, and that made me think she had something to hide. I'm afraid I was probably rather severe with her."

His admission he might have been too harsh surprised me, but then I had little on which to judge Weren, other than my brief introduction to him the other day. However, if Hydna was so enamoured as to risk her life for an affair with him, he must be a good man.

"I have already sent a runner for a healer," Panouk said, studying Ahmose with a frown. "I do apologise if this is a result of her interview. We are only trying to establish who has been using magic. There was no intention to harm anyone."

"We will look after her from here," I said. "Thank you for bringing her back, but we will not require you to stay."

I didn't expect they would want to linger any longer than necessary, and indeed, they both bowed and made to leave. Panouk gave Ahmose another worried look.

The apparent concern from both men for a mere servant surprised me. Panouk had always been polite enough, if overly officious, but had never shown any particular friendliness towards me. So his concern surprised me, even if as administrator he was responsible for the safety and wellbeing of the Palace's residents.

As Panouk and Weren left, they navigated around a woman who had just appeared in the doorway. She was perhaps ten years older than me and looked to be Egyptian. She carried a large basket filled with an assortment of clay pots and linen packets. There was no waiting to be invited in and she went straight to Ahmose, where she set down her basket and immediately began her examination, feeling Ahmose's skin, listening to her heart, and sniffing her breath.

We watched in silence. I was bemused at the way she didn't bother to introduce herself or so much as offer a greeting, but given Panouk himself had summoned her, perhaps she saw no need to waste time on such niceties.

Ahmose groaned again and tried to sit up. The healer put her hands on Ahmose's shoulders to stop her.

"Lie there a little longer, Old Mother," she said. "Allow me to finish my examination."

"I don't need an examination," Ahmose muttered. "I know exactly what is wrong with me."

"You do, do you?" the healer responded.

"It is my heart," Ahmose said. "I feel how hard it is working."

"Do you get light-headed?" the healer asked. "Dizzy?"

Ahmose closed her eyes again and nodded.

"Excessive tiredness?" the healer prompted.

Ahmose always seemed to be tired these days.

"She has been very pale," Ettu offered.

The healer acknowledged her words with a brief nod. She put her hands on Ahmose's chest and closed her eyes. Maybe she was counting Ahmose's heartbeats or listening to their pattern.

"How long has it been since you noticed these changes?" As she took Ahmose by the wrist, the old woman winced and the healer frowned. "Does your arm hurt?"

"I broke it not long ago," Ahmose said. "It is healed, but maybe I fell on it when I fainted."

The healer felt Ahmose's arm from wrist to shoulder.

"I don't think it is broken again," she said. "It is merely sprained. I will leave you a poultice to apply to it. You should be careful with that arm, though. It may be weak as a result of the break."

She took Ahmose's other arm and lay her fingers across her inner wrist.

"How long did you say it has been since you noticed the change in your heart?" she asked.

"A while," Ahmose said.

"Be more specific," the healer said.

"I started feeling more tired soon after we arrived in Egypt," Ahmose said. "I thought at first it might be a blood illness, but when my lungs started feeling like they were full of fluid, I knew it wasn't."

"I can give you a potion to help you breathe more easily," the healer said. "And something for the pain as it progresses. I am afraid there is probably nothing that can be done to strengthen your heart at this stage, though. I am sure you know how advanced your condition is."

Ahmose nodded, but didn't reply.

Tears welled and I went to stand at the window, looking out so nobody would notice. I had grown rather fond of the old woman in the time we had lived together. My feelings were a confusing mix of sadness at the discovery she was so ill, anger she hadn't told us, and disappointment in myself that I hadn't noticed. Yes, I had seen how pale she was, and her constant tiredness was obvious, but I hadn't thought to question it. Had just assumed it was a result of her advanced age. She must be well into her fifties, after all. She was probably the oldest woman I knew.

The healer left soon after, having provided Ahmose with a jar filled with herbs she mixed from the contents of her basket. They were to be steeped with hot water and drunk as a tea, she said. A linen packet contained more herbs for a poultice for Ahmose's arm, and she promised to send a runner with another mixture, as there was something else she hadn't brought with her that would be useful.

Ettu barred the door behind the healer and Sehener went off to retrieve Tall and Half. Ahmose made no attempt to get up, and Half dragged his little stool over to another couch. We all sat and looked at each other.

The silence in the chamber felt heavy and by the time it had stretched uncomfortably long, I didn't know how to break it.

"You may as well go ahead," Ahmose said at last. "I can feel you have something to say."

She turned her head and squinted in my direction.

"Why didn't you tell us?" I asked.

"It is nothing for anyone else to be concerned about." She started to sit up and Ettu quickly rose to help her.

"But of course we are concerned," Ettu said.

I hesitated, trying to find a response that didn't reveal my irritation. First, there was her daughter. Now, her health. How many other secrets did Ahmose hide? Fortunately Merytre spoke first, giving me more time to put my thoughts in order.

"What happened in your interview?" she asked.

How could I have forgotten that, even briefly?

"It didn't get far," Ahmose said. "Weren had only asked me a few questions before I fainted."

"What questions?" I asked. "And what did you tell him?"

"About my herbal knowledge, and I said only what I already told you I would say. He asked about what herb I would use for this or that condition."

"He was testing you," Ettu said.

"Yes," Ahmose said. "I gave him the correct answer for the first question, but made sure to muddle the second. If he has any herbal knowledge himself, he will recognise my error, although the herbs are similar enough that I doubt he will think it anything other than a genuine mistake."

"That was clever of you," Sehener said, her tone admiring.

"When he started asking about whether I knew any spells and whether I had ever tried to use magic, I could feel my heart beat faster," Ahmose said. "I was trying to calm myself, but then everything went black and the next thing I knew, I was being carried along the hallway."

"Teacher," Half said. "Have you considered they may think you faked such an episode to avoid being questioned further?"

Ahmose frowned. "A good point, but no, I don't think so. Panouk wouldn't have sent for a healer if he didn't believe it was genuine."

"Was it?" I asked. It hadn't even occurred to me before.

"Yes," Ahmose said. "Although I might have faked it had I thought of it. I admit I did play it up a little. I regained consciousness much sooner than they thought. It seemed prudent to feign ongoing unconsciousness, because no reasonable man would insist on continuing with the interview today if he believed me to be so unwell."

"So Weren will want to interview you again?" I asked.

Ahmose shrugged and leaned back against the couch, seemingly exhausted again.

"I suppose so. He strikes me as very determined." She stopped to catch her breath before continuing. "He does not seem like the sort of man who will let such an episode interfere with his investigation. I expect he will give me some time to recover, a day or two perhaps, then summon me again."

"Perhaps we should suggest he interviews you here next time," I said. "We could say it would be best if you don't have to walk so far."

"I think that sounds perfectly reasonable under the circumstances," Ettu said.

Ahmose made a movement that might have been a shrug. She didn't disagree, though.

"That is settled then," I said.

Ahmose didn't reply and seemed to have fallen asleep. I stifled a yawn, suddenly weary myself. I hadn't slept well last night and it seemed like a very good idea to lean back and close my eyes for a while.

CHAPTER 27

I looked down at my bed, where I myself lay, sleeping soundly. This must be a dream to observe myself in such a way, because even as I watched myself, I could still feel the cushion beneath my head and the linen sheet against my skin. It was confusing to be both in and above my body at the same time.

The door to my bedchamber burst open and two men entered. One of them tore away the sheet covering me. I woke, startled at first, then frightened.

"What are you doing?" I asked. "What do you want with me?"

Their only reply was a snarl. No, it was the growl of a lion. As I watched, the two men morphed into lions. The beasts dropped onto all fours and prowled around my bed. I suddenly held a single narcissus — somehow I knew it was the one Khaemmalu gave me and which was already wilted. It stood proudly in my fist now and I thrust it towards the lions. They snarled and moved back away from me.

I woke slowly, drifting through layers of grey, to find myself on the couch in the sitting chamber. My gaze went to the narcissus, still drooping in its mug. Merytre had commented earlier today that it was time to dispose of the blossom. I hadn't argued with her, but I was thankful she hadn't done it yet. The narcissus had protected me. It kept the lions from getting to me.

"Did you have a bad dream?" Ettu asked.

She was comfortably ensconced beside Half. They had moved back to their usual couch while I was asleep and he seemed to be dozing. Ahmose was in her favourite chair now, fast asleep, a soft snore coming from her open mouth. Tall and Sehener stood together at the window, both seemingly engrossed in whatever she was telling him. His shoulders shook a little as if he laughed.

"I suppose so," I said. "I hardly remember what it was now, though."

Ettu gave me a suspicious look as if she knew I lied, but didn't question me further. Ahmose stirred and Ettu turned her attention to her, fetching her some beer and asking if she needed a cushion or a footstool.

A runner boy arrived with the extra herbs from the healer. Ahmose set the jar aside and didn't seem inclined to use them.

"When are you going to take those?" I asked.

"Shall I send for hot water?" Merytre was already getting to her feet. "The healer said to brew them."

Ahmose waved at her to sit back down.

"Later," she said. "There is no hurry."

"Given the state you were in when they brought you back earlier, I would think there is," I said.

Ahmose gave me an even look.

"They will not provide any benefit," she said. "Not to me. My condition is too advanced."

"How do you know?" Ettu asked.

"Surely the healer wouldn't have told you to take it if she thought they wouldn't help," Sehener added.

"She likely felt she had to offer some remedy or other," Ahmose said. "I'm sure she could see as well as I can that it is pointless. My time to go to the West approaches and I have made my peace with that. The last thing I wanted from this life was to see my daughter again, and now I have done that, I can go to the afterlife feeling quite satisfied."

I blinked away the tears that welled as she spoke. The old woman was always there in her chair, sometimes joining in our conversations, but more often napping or busy with her own thoughts. She was a quiet, steady presence, but when she offered her opinion, it was always well considered. I valued her advice and her knowledge, but I hadn't realised I had grown to care for her as well, even if I didn't know how to describe our relationship. She was a friend, of sorts. Not a mother. Perhaps something like a grandmother.

"You mustn't give up." Sehener's voice was earnest and she leaned forward as she spoke, as if for emphasis. "Even if that one healer can't help you, there are others. Someone will be able to help."

"No, my dear." Ahmose gave her a pitying look. "I know quite enough to understand how dire the situation is. Don't fret for me. I am an old woman and have lived quite long enough."

"It isn't fair." Sehener wiped the tears from her cheeks. "You have only just found your daughter again. You deserve to have more time together before…"

Her voice choked and she stopped talking. Tall reached over to lay his hand on hers. They shared a look which seemed to steady her somewhat.

"I do hope you aren't all going to fuss like this until my time is over," Ahmose said, a little peevishly. "I have had quite enough of it already."

"It is only because we care about you," Ettu said. "Especially those of us who travelled here with you. You taught us so much on the ship. We wouldn't have adjusted so easily if not for you."

"You truly are very wise, Teacher," Half added. "I do believe you are quite the wisest person I have ever met."

"Me!" Tall said.

"That is enough from all of you." Ahmose's voice revealed her emotions, even if she was trying not to show it. "It is not like I'm going to immediately drop dead."

"I suppose we weren't expecting you to drop dead at all," I said.

I immediately regretted my comment and Sehener's gasp didn't make me feel any better. Ahmose didn't seem at all shocked.

"Well, now you do," she said. "And that is a good thing, because it gives you time to prepare yourselves. As for me, I am quite content with my lot. I am ready."

"Oh, Ahmose." Sehener went to her, bending over to hug the old woman.

Ahmose tolerated it for a few moments, then pushed her away.

"Quite enough," she said.

"Does Henuttawy know?" I asked.

A regretful look crossed Ahmose's face.

"No," she said. "I intend to tell her, but haven't yet found the right moment."

"She will probably hear about what happened today," Merytre pointed out. "You know how fast gossip spreads around here."

"I would be happy to take a message to her for you," Sehener said.

For a moment, Ahmose looked like she considered Sehener's offer, but she shook her head.

"Not yet," she said. "I have some time still and I would prefer to spend however long that may be getting to know my daughter again, not commiserating with her about my impending death."

"You should tell her soon," I said. "I am sure she would want time to prepare herself."

Time to say the things she would regret not saying, was what I really meant. The memory of that last conversation with Ishtar still hurt. The way I wondered whether she lied about being with child. That I never told her I loved her, regardless of the tension between us. That she died not knowing was something I would regret for the rest of my life.

The aroma of frankincense came to me again, but this time it was no more than a memory. Perhaps that's all it had been the other times too. No more than a fanciful thought, a wistful regret, a tangible expression of my longing to see my sister again. To speak with her one last time.

CHAPTER 28

To my great relief, Henutmire was in the dining chamber the following morning. I sat at the next table and tried not to stare at her while the serving women presented their trays to me. Her face was pale, but she was, as far as I could see, uninjured.

She waited only long enough for the serving women to depart before she leaned towards me.

"It is my brother," she said.

"Your brother?"

"The messenger from my father."

I hesitated, wondering whether I misunderstood. "Your father sent your brother to Pharaoh?"

"To see me with his own eyes."

Did Tiye know the messenger was Henutmire's brother? Was this another piece of information she had decided to keep to herself until she had a reason to reveal it?

"I begged Pharaoh to release him, but he says my father needs to learn that insolence won't be tolerated."

"Is he being treated well?" I hesitated to ask, but I couldn't imagine she wouldn't have sought this information from Pharaoh.

"So far," she said, although I didn't miss her worried frown. "I don't know how long Pharaoh will keep him here, though. I fear—"

A sob muffled the rest of whatever she said. I waited while she composed herself, sipping my goat milk and trying to look unbothered in case anyone watched. It was unlikely that Tiye was the only one who knew about Henutmire's brother, and no doubt speculation about the nature of our conversation would spread quickly, given her obvious distress.

"I fear Pharaoh will execute him," Henutmire continued at last. "To teach my father a lesson."

I sipped my milk to give myself a moment to think. How could I respond to that? Politely feign insistence that Pharaoh would never do such a thing? Or admit it was possible and risk upsetting Henutmire even more? But she didn't wait for my reply.

"I need you to send a letter for me," she said. "I must warn my father he has offended Pharaoh. He must stop asking about me."

"I have a maid who lives nearby," I said. "She can take it for you."

Henutmire gave me a grateful smile. "I will forward it to you this afternoon."

Back in my chambers, Merytre was quick to assure me that of course she would see Henutmire's letter into the hands of a courier.

When a runner came to say Weren was ready to continue Ahmose's interview, I told him to take back word that I had requested the interview be conducted in my chambers. For Ahmose's comfort, I said, and so I could ensure she did not become unwell again. Soon enough, Weren himself came knocking at the door.

"Thank you for accommodating my request," I said as he

seated himself in the chair we had positioned across from Ahmose.

He acknowledged me with a nod.

"It is unusual," he said, "and I do prefer to conduct such interviews in private, but given the circumstances, Panouk and I thought it best to allow it."

He shot a glance towards the other side of the chamber where Ettu, Merytre and Sehener had retreated. They stood looking out with their backs to us and appeared to be chatting amongst themselves, although I had no doubt that would stop as soon as the interview began. I thought Weren might ask them to leave, but it seemed they were far enough away to satisfy his requirement for privacy. He turned his attention to Ahmose.

"Let us continue then," he said, and his voice was kinder than I expected. "Are you ready?"

Ahmose nodded but didn't speak. She seemed to have little enough breath these days, so perhaps she saved it for her replies.

"Yesterday, we discussed your herbal knowledge," Weren said. "How you came to have this knowledge and the extent of it. Today I would like to discuss a sack which was found outside the Palace gates and which I have been reliably informed belongs to you. What can you tell me of this?"

"I have not lost any sacks since I arrived here," Ahmose said.

Her careful choice of words cheered me. Even if Weren had proof the sack was Ahmose's, as he alluded, and he knew how she came to be separated from it, he couldn't say she had lied. She never lost the sack in question. It was stolen from her.

"Tell me about the contents of the sack," Weren said.

"I am afraid that would be quite impossible," Ahmose said. "Since I have already told you I haven't lost a sack."

"How did your sack come to be outside the Palace gates when the administrators have no record of any request for you to leave?"

Ahmose already looked pale and I wondered whether I should

intervene. But the interview had barely started and Weren might think I tried to conceal something if I terminated it too soon.

"I'm sure I hardly need to point it out to you," she said. "But I have not requested permission to leave since I arrived here."

Weren frowned. He had, it seemed, noticed she was being deliberately obtuse with her answers.

"Tell me what you know about magic being used within the Palace," he said.

"To the best of my knowledge, nobody is currently using magic here."

Another answer that was as truthful as it was clever. She was seeking spells for me, but that wasn't the same as using them. And we weren't using her special potion at present either.

"What do you know about the strange events that occurred recently?" Weren asked. "Food spoiling unexpectedly fast. Objects being inexplicably lost. A flock of hens that died overnight."

"I am just a servant," Ahmose said. "I know only such as I have heard discussed in the hallways."

"And what is that?"

"A string of days that were unusually hot, even for *akhet*. Of course food will spoil easily. And folk misplace their belongings all the time."

Ahmose breathed more heavily now. Surely it was apparent to Weren that she couldn't continue for much longer.

"They can be careless, especially those who have an abundance. I suppose some of those items may have been stolen, but I expect most were merely misplaced and will be found at some point." She stopped to catch her breath. "As to the last, the hens, who knows what manner of sickness they may have developed? Someone with far more medical knowledge than me would have to examine the corpses to determine whether anything might be learned from their deaths."

By the time Ahmose got to the end of such a long speech, her face was grey and she panted.

"Weren, I'm afraid we must conclude your interview," I said. "Ahmose is not well enough to sustain much more."

He held up his hand, forefinger raised.

"Just one final question, if I may?" he asked.

I nodded. "Provided she can answer it briefly."

"Ahmose, what explanation can you give me for why these strange events ceased as soon as I began investigating them?" Weren asked.

Ahmose's eyelids fluttered and she slumped in her chair as if about to lose consciousness. I jumped up and went to her.

"That is enough," I said. "This is more than she can handle in such a frail state. I think she has already answered your final question anyway. Given she has said she knows nothing of magic use, she can hardly have any explanation for the cessation of such magic."

Ettu, Merytre and Sehener must have been listening because they came to crowd around Ahmose, quite neatly blocking Weren from her. Ettu brought her some beer, Sehener propped her feet up on a stool, and Merytre patted her on the arm.

"Very well then." Weren got to his feet.

I studied his face, trying to determine whether he was satisfied with the outcome of their discussion, but he gave no sign of his thoughts.

"I trust that will be the final time you need to interview her," I said.

"For now," he said. "I may have some further questions for her at a later stage, as I have yet to establish the circumstances of the sack that apparently belongs to her, but that will do for now."

He headed towards the door and I followed him into the hallway.

"Weren," I said. "Ahmose has been most insistent the sack is not hers. Why do you not believe her?"

He gave me a frank look.

"I have been told by someone who I have no reason to disbelieve that it does indeed belong to her," he said. "Until Ahmose can offer evidence to the contrary, I am afraid I will continue to hold that position."

"Who exactly told you this?" I asked.

"Henuttawy," he said. "She is lady's maid to Lady Tiye."

CHAPTER 29

*A*hmose would be devastated if she knew it was Henuttawy who told Weren about her sack. And I was furious. If Henuttawy knew, it could only be because Ahmose had told her, and whatever Henuttawy knew, Tiye probably did too. They both knew more than they should, and far more than I had realised.

Before I went back inside, I took a couple of deep breaths to compose myself and arranged my face into an expression I hoped wouldn't reveal I had just learned something startling. As I took my seat again, I resolved to keep my mouth shut until I had sorted through my thoughts.

How much did Tiye know? About Tall and Half? About our journey to the House of Life? Had she been toying with me all this time while I sat in her chamber and earnestly tried to develop a friendship with her?

"That seemed to go well enough," Ettu said to me, even as she continued to fuss over Ahmose.

I only nodded, knowing that if I tried to speak right now, far more than I meant to say would come tumbling out.

"I don't understand why he is so sure the sack belongs to Ahmose," Merytre said.

I clamped my mouth shut. I wouldn't be the one to reveal to Ahmose her daughter's betrayal.

"Should I send for the healer?" Sehener asked.

Ahmose shook her head, but didn't seem to be able to speak. She still breathed far too heavily and her face was an alarming shade of grey.

"Yes," I said. "Find a runner and tell him to hurry."

Ahmose waved her hand at me.

"Not… necessary," she gasped.

"Don't—" I mimicked her hand wave "—at me. Surely the healer can do something to make you more comfortable."

Ahmose gestured towards the table where the healer's herbs waited, the jars still unopened. The only one she had used so far was the packet of poultice herbs. I supposed what she was trying to say was that the healer had already done what she could. All the woman could do now was reiterate that Ahmose should take the mixtures she had prepared.

"Sehener, send for hot water," I said. "If Ahmose does not want the healer to return, then she will take the herbs as she was instructed to."

Ahmose shot me a look, but didn't argue. I supposed she figured it was the better of the two options.

Sehener hurried away and soon returned with news that a runner was on his way to the kitchen. She slipped down to the mens' bedchamber to let them know they would have to stay in there a little longer. There was no point letting them out now, only to lock them away again so soon.

When the water arrived, Merytre steeped the herbs before she brought it to Ahmose. I watched carefully to ensure the old woman actually drank the potion, not just sat holding it until the water cooled, but she sipped it almost immediately. By the time the mug was empty, she seemed to breathe a little easier and her face was a more normal colour. So, the herbs apparently had some effect, despite her insistence they would do nothing for her.

By this time, Panouk had come knocking. With the men safely locked away again, Merytre let him in. Given the early termination of Ahmose's second interview, I was hardly surprised to see him.

"Administrator." I greeted him with a stern look. "I hope you aren't here to continue Weren's interview. Ahmose is really not well enough for it at present."

"Actually, I came to speak with you." He cast his gaze over the other women, then turned back to me. "In private, if I may."

Ahmose moved as if to get up, but I gestured for her to stay where she was.

"We can talk outside," I said.

As we stood in the hallway, Panouk cleared his throat. He seemed uncomfortable, which surprised me. I had thought perhaps he wanted to confirm a date for my own interview with Weren.

"Did you want something?" I asked when he didn't seem inclined to begin the conversation.

"Weren has shared his observations with me," he said. "About his interview with Ahmose."

"And what might that be?" I gave him what I hoped was an unconcerned look.

"He is convinced she knows more than she is saying," he said. "However, her medical condition is interfering in his attempts to interview her."

"I'm afraid I must insist there be no further interviews," I said. "As Weren has already seen, Ahmose is not well enough for such a thing. I fear the pressure of such interviews will exacerbate her heart condition."

"Your concern for your servant does you credit, my lady." He had said something similar once before, but this time, he actually sounded sincere. He hesitated, as if choosing his words with care.

"My lady, I need to ask you a question and I hope you will give me an honest answer."

"I will give you the most honest answer I can."

It seemed to be enough for him.

"Do you have any reason to doubt your servant's loyalty?" he asked.

"Ahmose? Of course not."

He studied my face, clearly waiting for something more.

"She travelled with me from Babylon," I said. "She taught me your language and your customs. She has been an invaluable aid and ally to me here."

"That may be," he said. "But are you certain you can trust her? The reason I ask…" He paused, as if searching for a delicate way to express his thought. "Many plots and plans are laid in a place of this magnitude. You likely know any number of people here who you cannot trust, whether you know it or not. I am asking how certain you are of Ahmose."

"Absolutely certain," I said. "There is no doubt in my mind she is entirely loyal."

But Henuttawy knew about the stolen sack, and maybe more. Did I really know Ahmose as well as I thought? I shouldn't reveal my doubts to Panouk, though. Ahmose would surely have a good explanation.

"Was there anything else, Administrator?" I asked, when he seemed to hesitate.

"I hope you know, Lady Kassaya." He stopped to clear his throat and looked distinctly uncomfortable now. "You can trust me. I realise we did not get off to the most fortuitous of starts, but you can come to me if there is anything you need."

He looked directly at me as he spoke and I sensed no duplicity in either his face or his tone. We had thought at one point Panouk might be involved in the matter of the disappearing women. I no longer believed that, but he wasn't willing to listen when I expressed my doubt about Amankhau. That alone gave me reason to hesitate.

"I tried to bring a concern to you once before," I reminded him. "You told me you didn't want to know."

He shuffled his feet and looked away for a moment.

"You caught me off-guard that day," he said, looking back at me. "But I am an ally to you, whether you believe it or not. If you have evidence of something that should be investigated, I hope you would bring it to me before anyone else."

"Even if it is about someone in a position of power within the Palace?"

He held my gaze and didn't even blink.

"Yes," was all he said.

"Very well, then. Should I have evidence of what I suspect, I will come to you, and I will expect you to take me seriously."

"You have my word," he said.

CHAPTER 30

*P*anouk hadn't even left the hallway before a runner boy came hurtling towards me, his chest puffed up with the significance of his message. I had seen runners bursting with self-importance enough times to know it probably meant a message from Pharaoh, and I braced myself.

It surely meant he wanted to see me. Maybe to finally chastise me for fleeing from him. I would have to act contrite. Pretend I didn't hate him with every fibre of my being. Pretend I didn't know he had killed my sister and countless others. Act like I thought him to be a living god, as the folk here believed. He would still be angry about the way our *senet* game ended. I might have to grovel to placate him. The very idea disgusted me.

But the boy's message wasn't to summon me to merely dine with Pharaoh. I was required to attend a festival with him as an honoured wife.

"Which other Ornaments will be there?" I asked the boy, fully expecting he wouldn't answer.

To my surprise, he obliged me with a reply.

"The Queen is unable to attend, so the Lady Tiye will take her place at Pharaoh's side," he said.

I blinked at him, too surprised to formulate a response. He probably wouldn't have answers for the questions it raised for me anyway. I nodded a dismissal at him, and he hurried away.

Back in my chambers, I barred the door and everyone looked at me expectantly. I could hardly share Panouk's words with them, but I had to give them something.

"I am to attend a festival with Pharaoh next week," I said instead, hoping the news would distract them from Panouk.

Sehener gave a startled "oh" and Merytre looked impressed. Ettu shrugged at me, clearly having no more information than I did as to how important this was.

"I suppose he means the festival to honour Min," Merytre said.

"I don't believe I have heard that name before," I said.

Min must be a deity, but I didn't even know whether they were a god or a goddess.

"He is the god of fertility," she said. "Also of harvests. I suppose you have been invited because you carry Pharaoh's babe."

"Very symbolic." Ettu nodded her approval.

"Tiye is to attend as well," I said. "In place of the queen."

Ettu's eyebrows shot up, but neither Merytre nor Sehener seemed fazed by this news.

"Lady Tiye sometimes attends festivals with Pharaoh," Merytre said. "Although, I don't believe I have ever heard of her doing so when the queen has also been in attendance. I think it is more that she takes the queen's place at times."

When I first came to Egypt, I expected to be queen myself. How naive I was. I soon realised Pharaoh already had a queen, but also that if she died, Tiye was the obvious choice to replace her. My father knew I wouldn't be queen, and so had my sister. Neither had bothered to tell me.

"Should we arrange a new gown for you, my lady?" Sehener's voice was eager and I tried to stifle my groan.

"I don't—" I started, but Ettu and Merytre launched into a discussion about possibilities, drowning out my attempted protest.

The gown would have to suit the blue sapphire from Pharaoh, of course, they said, but must be sufficiently different from the last gown made to match the gem.

I busied myself with my thoughts while they discussed potential designs. There was no need for my opinion. The gown would be perfectly suitable without any input from me. Indeed, any of my maids could probably arrange a gown magnificent enough for such a festival. Except perhaps Abar. She had shown little interest in integrating herself with the folk here and I doubted she paid enough attention to Egyptian fashions to have any idea what such a gown should be like.

But then, she had no reason to integrate herself, as she had repeatedly pointed out. She was brought to Egypt against her will, and now her sister was dead, a circumstance she seemed to blame me for. Ettu and Merytre had warned I should have Abar dismissed for the hostility she showed towards me, or at least have her transferred.

I had a lot of sympathy for the girl, though. After all, her situation was not all that different from mine, other than our relative statuses. So I allowed her to stay in my service, despite the threats she had made against me after learning of her sister's death.

The earthy aroma of frankincense filled my nostrils, as if thinking about the death of a sister had summoned Ishtar to the chamber. I couldn't stop myself from looking for her, but of course, she wasn't here. There was nobody here other than those I expected to see: Ettu, Merytre and Sehener, along with Tall and Half. Ahmose had gone to lie down in her bedchamber while I was outside with Weren.

I breathed deeply of the fragrance, trying to find a rational explanation for it. None of my close companions wore such a perfume — indeed, it was too expensive for a servant as my maids had pointed out — and it was not a scent they had ever used on me, preferring instead to douse me in the floral scents that irritated my nose.

I didn't know of any flowers with a fragrance that might be mistaken for frankincense, and the only flower in my chambers at present was the single narcissus from Khaemmalu, now wilted and hanging over the side of the mug.

There was nothing we ate or drank that had a similar aroma. I really didn't have any explanation, other than the one I had barely let myself consider. That I kept smelling Ishtar's perfume because her spirit still lingered in the mortal realm.

CHAPTER 31

The week leading up to the festival passed slowly with little other than the dress fittings to occupy me. I managed to see Khaemmalu twice, and the physician came again to examine me. Sutem had provided us with the items Tall needed to build a privacy screen. He fashioned a wooden frame to which he attached a length of linen, and it did indeed give me some measure of privacy during the physician's visits.

On one of her better days, I asked Ahmose what I should expect of the festival for Min. Apparently there would be a parade and she thought I could expect a place of honour towards the front of the procession. A statue of Min would be displayed, and there would be musicians and maybe even acrobats. People would line the streets to see Pharaoh and his queen, or in this case Tiye, pass by.

It sounded chaotic and noisy, and in truth, I dreaded it, not least because it would be the first time I had seen Pharaoh since our disastrous *senet* game. I hated the thought of being paraded in such a way. They would stare at me, not that anyone watching the parade would know who I was. I would be just another anonymous wife of Pharaoh, if they even knew that much.

When the day of the festival arrived, I woke with my stomach churning. My maids came earlier than usual to prepare me, because apparently the preparations for such an event would be even longer and more tedious than usual. I endured their attentions without comment and tried not to hear their excited chatter, because it made me even more nervous.

Despite my attempts to block out their conversation, it was hard not to hear at least some of it. Apparently Khensa and Tuya had received permission to watch the parade. Hemetre was upset because it hadn't occurred to her that she might be able to go and now it was too late to ask.

The others were excited at being given a half day off in celebration and chatted about how they planned to spend their precious time off. Only Abar didn't comment. As usual, she waited by the door and said nothing unless directly spoken to. She didn't even glare at me, which I was grateful for, even if I wondered why.

The gown designed for me to wear today was elaborate and far too fussy for my taste. It clung to my newly protruding belly in a way I particularly disliked. I had tried protesting this feature, but apparently because Min was the god of fertility, and I was undoubtedly invited on account of the babe, everyone except me agreed the gown should highlight my belly. It also dipped low over my chest, with barely more than a couple of thin straps to cover my breasts, another factor that made me exceedingly uncomfortable. I didn't remember the fabric being quite so meagre when I tried it on while it was still being stitched.

"My lady, it is so exciting to see you finally showing," Khensa said, her fingertips brushing the side of my belly as she straightened the gown.

I was so surprised, it took me too long to find a reply and by then, others were also commenting.

"Oh my, I can't wait for everyone to realise," Tuya said.

"I have never served an Ornament who carried Pharaoh's

babe before," Hemetre said with a giggle. "Everyone will be so jealous."

They continued with their chatter, sounding ever more merry. Of course, they would have realised I was with child. Given they saw me naked every day, they could hardly have avoided noticing the changes to my body. And, it finally dawned on me, they must have seen the tray of barley and emer. Those who were raised in Egypt would have understood the significance of the sprouting barley without needing to be told.

What I didn't understand was why they hadn't commented before. Perhaps they had waited for me to tell them, or maybe they waited until it became unavoidably obvious, as in this gown.

I waited until the maids left, still chattering excitedly about their plans for the afternoon, before I gestured for Ettu to come closer. I was embarrassed enough without everyone hearing me.

"I don't remember the gown being quite like this," I said.

She frowned as she eyed me up and down.

"You tried it on three times," she said. "What is not to your liking?"

"This." I gestured towards my chest.

She shrugged, the gesture clearly indicating she didn't know what I meant.

"I don't remember there being so little fabric," I said.

"We might have adjusted the design slightly after you last tried it on."

"They are not your breasts on display," I grumbled.

"The gown is perfectly decent. You know folk here think little of displaying their bodies."

"What if my breasts fall out the side?" I asked. "There is barely enough fabric to cover them, let alone hold them, and they seem bigger than they used to be."

"Hmm." Ettu eyed my chest in a way that made me feel like a prize cow being traded. "I think it will be fine. You will probably be in a palanquin most of the time. After all, they will hardly make you walk, not in your condition. Just sit up straight and keep your arms at your sides. If you must wave, use your lower arms."

I sighed. It sounded too complicated and all because nobody was willing to let me have a little more fabric at the front. At least my belly wouldn't be so visible if I was seated.

Pharaoh's sapphire was a heavy lump at my throat. I hated wearing the dark blue gem. It was too heavy and every moment I wore it was a reminder it was a reward for getting myself with child. As if I could will my body to conceive. Or as if Pharaoh had willed it.

Sehener and Merytre walked me to the front gates where my transport waited. A guard helped me into the palanquin and I clamped my arms to my sides, mindful of Ettu's instructions. At a shout from their master, the slaves lifted the palanquin onto their shoulders and we set off.

The air held a festive buzz even before we reached the palace. There were more folk on the streets than was usual for midday, and those who were out and about seemed particularly cheery. A trio of little girls dashed down the street, holding aloft ribbons which unfurled behind them as they ran. A pair of boys sparred with sticks.

"I am the god, Min," one cried as we passed them. "And I will win every battle, because today is my festival day."

His opponent seemed undaunted by his god-like state and smacked him smartly on the top of his head. The boy's indignant howls trailed away as we left them behind.

The palanquin slowed as we approached Pharaoh's palace and the streets became clogged with folk. The slave master positioned himself in front and gestured importantly for folk to stand aside.

"Make way, make way," he cried. "An Ornament of Pharaoh approaches. Make way for the wife of Pharaoh."

He sounded officious and folk were quick to scurry out of the way. They eyed me curiously as we passed. I caught the gaze of a young woman who must have been no older than me. She held a newborn, jiggling the babe as she watched my approach. A purple bruise spread around one eye and I wondered if it was her husband who had caused it.

There was something about her face that made me think we might have been friends, if circumstances were different. If I hadn't been in a palanquin, I might have stopped, but then we were past her and heading deeper into the crowd. I looked back over my shoulder to see her turn to watch me depart. I gave her a little smile and a startled expression crossed her face before she tentatively returned it.

When we reached the Palace, the slaves lowered the palanquin. I started to stand, expecting to get out, but a guard waved at me to sit back down.

"Stay there please, my lady," he said. "We will be leaving very shortly and it will be more efficient if you are already seated."

My backside was numb and an ache in my calf felt like it would turn into a cramp if I couldn't stretch my leg, but there was no point telling him. His attention had already shifted away from me, as if he had more important things to do than watch over an Ornament. I sat back down and stretched my leg in front of me to ease the ache.

We waited for some time — certainly it would have been long enough for me to have stood for a while, perhaps even taken a short walk — before the order came to move on. It was only once I was in the air again, that I saw a second palanquin. The sunlight bouncing off the gold plating indicated this must be Pharaoh's.

As we drew closer, I saw Pharaoh did indeed ride in the golden palanquin and beside him sat Tiye. She looked truly beautiful in a silvery white gown. Her braids were twisted up and pinned to her crown, with a silver circlet set on top. She caught my eye and gave me what seemed to be a pointed look. Then she smiled at me, a broad beam that felt completely impersonal.

Perhaps she was telling me I should try harder to look happy about being here.

Somewhere out of my sight, musicians struck up a cheery tune filled with trumpets and flutes and the crash of cymbals. The palanquins set off and, to my surprise, I found I travelled directly behind Pharaoh and Tiye. This was indeed a place of honour.

The procession moved at a leisurely place. The street down which we paraded was lined on both sides with folk, all dressed in what must surely be their finest, even if it was often ragged or in need of mending.

Every now and then, I glimpsed the line of soldiers who marched ahead of Pharaoh's palanquin. They carried a standard, or maybe it was a flag. Fabric streamed out from it and rippled in the breeze. Perhaps they also bore the statue of Min that Ahmose said would be displayed.

The crowds lining the streets seemed endless. They cheered and smiled, and children held up ribbons, letting them flutter in the breeze. I waved with my upper arms clasped firmly to my sides. A trio of young girls tossed flowers in my direction.

All I saw as they came towards me was a blur of yellow. One landed on my lap and it was only then I saw it was a narcissus. I stared at it for a moment, not wanting to touch it, but the girls were watching me. When I held the flower aloft, they jumped up and down and hugged each other. The slaves kept marching and soon enough, we were past the girls.

I threw the narcissus on the floor of the palanquin and wiped my fingers on the fabric covering the bench. I didn't want to touch a narcissus. Not today when I would probably speak with Pharaoh. There was no room in my head today for the mystery of whatever the flowers were trying to tell me.

CHAPTER 32

By the time the palanquin drew to a halt, my cheeks were sore from smiling and I had long given up waving. My transport hit the ground a little too heavily and the slave master barked a reprimand. A guard came to hold my hand and help me out.

We had stopped just behind a dais on which stood two golden thrones, shaded by a striped awning. Pharaoh already sat on the larger throne, his feet propped up on a footstool. A servant brought him a goblet, which he took without even so much as a glance at her.

Tiye had stopped to adjust her skirts, but now she made her way up the three steps to the dais. The train of her gown trailed behind her. She sat beside Pharaoh and the serving woman was swift to offer her a drink. My mouth was dry and I looked forward to some refreshments.

"You may sit here, my lady," the guard said, directing me to a spot beside the dais.

The place allocated to me had no shade, but someone had at least been thoughtful enough to provide a stool for me. The guard took up position beside me, his stance indicating he expected to be there for some time. Perhaps he was assigned to keep watch over me.

Folk were rowdy by now, and many carried mugs or bottles of wine, which they had clearly been imbibing from. A ring of guards around the dais kept them at a distance and I was thankful to be included within their sphere. I craned my neck looking for the serving woman and hoped she was on her way to me, but from where I sat, I couldn't see her. I started to stand, meaning to wave to draw her attention, but the guard beside me was quick to stop me.

"Please stay seated, my lady," he said. "A crowd like this can be unpredictable and it is far easier to protect you if you do as we say."

"Of course."

I sat down and tried not to notice the dryness of my throat or the way my stomach grumbled. I had time to eat no more than a few bites of bread before my maids arrived this morning. To distract myself, I examined my surroundings. The ring of guards mostly blocked my view and I couldn't see much past them. Within their circle, and within my line of sight, was the dais, and Pharaoh and Tiye on the golden thrones.

What did Tiye think about as she sat beside Pharaoh? Had she done this enough times that it was routine, or was it still exciting? Did she war with herself about playing the devoted wife despite what she knew about him? I couldn't imagine how it would feel to sit there as if I was queen, even if it was beside a man I despised more than anyone else in the world.

Pharaoh glanced over at her and Tiye gave him a look which could only be described as adoring. How did she hide her feelings so well? My anger and resentment boiled so furiously within me that surely everyone could feel it.

As soon as Pharaoh's attention was off her, Tiye's gaze focused on something a little to her left. I craned my neck to see what it was, hoping for a distraction from my dry throat and empty belly. She seemed to watch a particular young man. I had only a partial view of him, not much more than the side of his head and one shoulder, but I recognised Tiye in the way he held himself. It must be her son, Pentaweret.

Maybe that would be me one day. Sitting beside Pharaoh at some festival the queen couldn't attend. Soaking in every glimpse of my son. Observing who he spoke to and his manner as he did. Perhaps hearing a snatch of his words, his voice, his laugh. Storing away all those glimpses, knowing it would have to last me until whenever I saw him again.

A woman's squeal interrupted my thoughts and I strained to see what had happened. The crowd was drawing back away from something. I leaned forward for a better look, clutching the sides of the stool to avoid embarrassing myself by falling off. As the folk parted, I finally saw the cause of the disturbance.

A cobra, raised as if to strike, swayed from side to side. In front of the snake sat an old man blowing into what might have been a reed pipe. As the noise of the crowd briefly dipped, I caught a snatch of a tune, high and thin. I had seen snake charmers before and always found myself as entranced with them as their snakes seemed to be.

The man swayed, matching the cobra's movements as if they danced together. He seemed unconcerned by the peril of being so close to such a deadly creature. How did he convince the snake to do that? Did it live with him in his home? Had it ever bitten him? So many questions ran through my mind as I watched the two of them.

It was only when movement in front of the dais indicated the beginning of the ceremony, that the man reached out to the cobra. I held my breath as the cobra dipped its head towards his sleeve, then disappeared up it. I waited for any sign it had bitten him, but the man seemed completely comfortable. If I hadn't seen the cobra slide right up his sleeve, I wouldn't have looked twice at him, except he was the only man in the area wearing a shirt.

The ceremony itself was long and tedious. Priests presented offerings to Pharaoh and said lengthy prayers which seemed to be both to and about him. Pharaoh, it seemed, was treated with as much importance as the god the festival was supposed to celebrate.

A brazier in front of the dais sent the sweet smell of incense wafting through the air, tickling my throat. I suppressed my cough, although my eyes watered with the effort. I didn't dare rub them for fear of smudging my kohl.

Two priests brought the statue of Min from a cabinet carried on its own small palanquin. They held the god carefully and with great reverence for the crowd to view. Given how casual the Egyptians were about nudity, I shouldn't have been shocked to see the god's phallus, which was half as long as the statue was high.

It took me some time to realise the young man who took a leading role in the ceremony must be Pharaoh's son and heir, Ramses. I glanced at Tiye, looking for some clue as to how she felt about seeing him like this, but she wasn't watching Ramses. I didn't need to be able to see what she looked at to know it must be her son.

As a priest began yet another lengthy prayer, I let my gaze roam over the crowd. Young, old, rich, poor. They were all here today. Some seemed to watch the ceremony with avid fascination, while others appeared as bored as I felt. More than one babe cried as his mother bounced him in her arms. I was only half-listening when my own name jolted me back into awareness of the ceremony.

The voice of a man I couldn't see — presumably another priest — described me as an Ornament of Pharaoh, the daughter of a beloved ally, a Princess of Babylon. All terms I would have expected. It was only when he went on to say that I carried the child of Pharaoh that I froze.

The noise around me dimmed and faded as I realised my babe

was now public knowledge. No longer was he a secret, known only by a select handful of folk. Suddenly, everyone knew.

And that meant Khaemmalu would undoubtedly know before the night was over. Word of something so important would travel swiftly. I should have told him when I had the chance.

I barely noticed the rest of the ceremony as I tried to figure out how to explain to Khaemmalu. If I could find him as soon as I returned to the Palace, I might have a chance of telling him myself before the gossip reached him. There was no more time to find the right words to tell the man I loved that I carried someone else's babe.

The priests droned on and on. My mouth was parched, my stomach growled, I longed to relieve myself, and I desperately needed to get to Khaemmalu before the gossip did. And still there was no sign of the ceremony ending.

At long last, Ramses finished his monologue, which was almost as interminable as if it was delivered by Pharaoh himself. I barely heard his speech, too busy worrying about the fact that every moment I sat here was another moment in which someone might be telling Khaemmalu about the babe.

When Ramses finally stopped talking, I held in my sigh, expecting it would be Pharaoh's turn next and I would have to sit through another lengthy speech. But, no, it seemed the ceremony was over.

My guard signalled I could get up. I tried not to groan as I got to my feet. My behind was numb, my back ached, and my bladder was about to burst.

"Pharaoh will see you now," the guard said.

This time I couldn't stop the groan from escaping my lips. If the guard noticed, he pretended not to. I approached the dais, wondering if I would be expected to prostrate myself. Marduk damn me, but I would not lie on my belly in front of Tiye as if she was a queen.

But Pharaoh must have been distracted — indeed, from his

hand high on Tiye's thigh, I guessed his thoughts had little to do with Min — because he gave me his usual blank look that seemed to signify he didn't know who I was.

I stared at his feet while I waited. It was better than looking him in the eyes. The golden sandals he wore encapsulated fat toes and his ankles bulged in a way that was surely painful. There was truly nothing attractive about this man. Not even his feet.

When I glanced up to see why he hadn't yet spoken, his gaze was on the blue sapphire at my throat.

"You wore it this time," he said.

So, he hadn't entirely forgotten me, but maybe he didn't remember it was me he played *senet* with. Or perhaps I wasn't the only Ornament he had played with lately and he couldn't recall which had angered him. Was it possible he really didn't remember most of his "wives", except a favoured few?

"It was a most generous gift," I said. "My lord."

His gaze drafted downwards. My cheeks heated at the casual way he inspected my body and I wished again the gown put less focus on my belly.

"My physician has been to see you?" he asked.

"Yes, of course." Perhaps the son I carried mattered to him, even if he claimed otherwise. "He said everything is progressing well."

"Good." He looked away, a clear indication I was dismissed.

I left before he could change his mind.

CHAPTER 33

As I entered the Palace grounds, the only thought on my mind was Khaemmalu. His name echoed in time with my heartbeats. There was no time left to figure out the best way to tell him. The right words didn't matter anymore. I just needed to tell him before he heard from someone else. Why in Marduk's name didn't I do it earlier?

The sun was still sinking towards the horizon. Despite how endless the ceremony had seemed, it was probably too early for Khaemmalu to be on duty yet. Unless he came early tonight. He knew I was attending the festival, so maybe he would be early in the hope of seeing me as I returned.

I wandered the path where I most commonly encountered him, but there was no sign of Khaemmalu. No matter, it wasn't even dark yet. He would find me sooner or later. But although I walked until the sun was fully set, he still didn't appear. He would definitely be at work by now, so he must be avoiding me.

The dryness in my throat was increasingly difficult to ignore and my stomach grumbled fiercely. I had stopped in a hidden spot to relieve myself, so at least that discomfort was gone. Eventually, I turned back. There was no point wandering around out here all night. Perhaps he was busy, or he had decided for whatever reason not to reveal himself. I didn't let myself think of the possibility he might have already heard my news.

I was almost back at the torch-lit path that led up to the Palace when I got the sense that someone watched me. I squared my shoulders and walked on. It could be any of the guards, and if it was Khaemmalu, he would or he wouldn't reveal himself. It was his choice. I had made myself available by being here. A bush next to the path rustled.

"Kassaya." His voice was as calm as ever, but it had an unfamiliar undertone. "Back here."

As I slipped between the bushes, he was suddenly there in front of me. Normally he would take my hand to lead me, but tonight he only turned and walked ahead of me.

"Follow me," he said.

Oh, Marduk, he knew. There was no other reason he wouldn't touch me.

With my heart beating so loudly, he must surely hear it, I followed. At length, he stopped and turned. In the depths of the shadows, I could make out no more than his silhouette, but I felt the way his eyes bored into me.

"Why didn't you tell me?" was all he said.

I burst into tears. I didn't mean to, but somehow when he asked me that, it was all I could do. He waited silently while I cried.

"I wanted to," I said when the tears finally slowed. "I have been trying to find the right way to tell you, but it was so hard, and I kept thinking it could wait until next time. I didn't know there would be an announcement. I would have told you. I wanted to tell you myself."

A chill emanated from him. He was angry with me. No, worse. He was furious.

"Khaemmalu," I started, but I could feel how he withdrew from me even before he spoke.

"You should go inside," he said. "You have had a long day."

"I don't want to leave you," I said. "Not like this, with this… thing between us."

"Just go, Kassaya." His voice was weary now. "I need to think."

I headed back to the path. There was no point arguing with him and I could hardly blame him for wanting some time. He had never asked whether I had lain with Pharaoh, but he must surely have assumed I had. Nevertheless, the news of my babe obviously came as a shock. Why didn't I tell him when I had the chance?

As I emerged from the shrubbery, a figure stood right in front of me. My heart jumped as I stopped. Khaemmalu is nearby, I told myself. He won't let anything happen to me, no matter how mad he is.

As my eyes adjusted to the relative brightness of the moonlight, I recognised her. She stood beside the path, facing the place where I had emerged from the shrubbery. As if she knew I was in there and knew exactly where I would come out.

"Were you waiting for me?" I hoped my voice was steady enough to not reveal my shock at encountering her.

"I think it is more you who waited for me," she said.

The moonlight was dim tonight and the scales on her face were no more than a shimmer. Irritation sparked within me at her obscure answer. If she had a message for me, why didn't she just say it? I was tired of her cryptic responses.

"Do you ever give a straight answer?" I asked.

She tipped her head to the side, studying me.

"You have yet to ask the right question," she said.

"What is the right question then? Tell me and I will gladly ask it."

The ghost of a smile crossed her face, then disappeared as quickly as it came.

"You are still not paying attention," she said.

"I'm listening." I poured all the sincerity I could into my voice.

As frustrating as I found her cryptic statements, I did want to understand her message, whatever it was.

"The answer you seek is in front of you," she said. "Or, rather, right now, it is behind you."

Then she turned and walked away. She crossed the path, heading into the shrubbery on the other side.

"Wait," I said.

"May Sekhmet protect you," she said over her shoulder.

Then she was gone.

Her words drifted on the wind. *The answer you seek is behind you,* she had said. What was behind me? Shrubbery, darkness, shadows.

And Khaemmalu.

CHAPTER 34

My thoughts warred between the conversation with the seer and Khaemmalu's anger. At least the distraction of the seer meant I didn't reach my chambers in tears as I would have if I'd had nothing other than Khaemmalu to think about.

I must have looked very somber, because Merytre didn't say a word when she opened the door. I poured myself some beer. In my distress at Khaemmalu's reaction, I had almost forgotten how very thirsty I was. Everyone was in the sitting chamber, even Ahmose, although she still looked paler than she should. Well, almost everyone.

"Where are Tall and Sehener?" I asked.

Ettu stammered and blushed, and it was Merytre who answered.

"In her bedchamber, I assume," she said with a laugh. "The last time I looked down the hallway, her door was closed, so I wasn't going to go in and find out."

I drained my mug and refilled it, then went to sit down. I didn't need to ask what they might be doing in there. How nice to have the luxury of a door to close and a bed to lie on. It made me wonder whether Ettu and Half also slipped away together like that when I wasn't here. I glanced at Ettu in time to see her giving Half a furtive smirk. I supposed that answered my question.

"Has there been any more word from Weren?" I asked.

"Nothing today," Ettu said, "and none of us went out while you were gone, so the only news we have is whatever we learned this morning."

My maids had brought with them the usual inconsequential gossip. I rarely bothered to listen to it.

"You never did teach me how to make your special potion," I said to Ahmose. I had meant it as an offhand remark, but my tone sounded more accusatory than I intended and I hurried to remedy it. "I suppose that is a good thing now with Weren's investigation."

"It is," Ahmose said, "although it was not a deliberate decision on my part." She paused to catch her breath. "The time was never right and then I used the last of the key herb. There was no point teaching you without that."

"I suppose it might not be possible for you to get more of that again," I said. "Whoever was supplying you will probably be more cautious from now on."

"Perhaps," she admitted. "Although she never knew what I used it for. She may suspect it was for a spell of some sort, but it would be no more than a suspicion."

"Who is she?" I asked. "You have never even told me that much."

She only looked at me and I knew she wouldn't tell me the woman's name no matter how many times I asked.

"Henuttawy," Ettu said. "Isn't it?"

"It is," Ahmose said. She gave no sign of whether she was disappointed or relieved Ettu had figured it out.

Of course it would be her daughter. Why didn't I think of that? Ahmose would have started teaching Henuttawy what she knew as soon as the girl was old enough to understand. It must have been enough to instil a thirst for knowledge in the young girl, which continued even past being taken from her mother.

And now I knew why she wouldn't reveal her source earlier, even though I didn't know Henuttawy was her daughter back then. She probably feared I would mention it to Tiye, who might then reveal enough for me to figure out their connection.

Ahmose said nothing further, but then she wasn't one to apologise for keeping such a thing from me. What other secrets did she have? It was too late to wonder whether I could really trust her. She already knew everything being concealed within the walls of my chambers.

Well, almost everything. She didn't know about my relationship with Khaemmalu, or she might know whatever guesses the other women had shared with her, but none of them truly knew what was between him and I. None of them knew I loved him, and that was something I would keep to myself. Especially now, when I didn't know whether he would ever want to be with me again. I couldn't bear to think of how alone I would be without him. Time seemed so precious now my sister was gone. I hoped he wouldn't waste too much time being angry with me.

The thought of Ishtar reminded me of the little lioness I found on the banks of the pleasure lake. I fished it out of my pouch and turned the figure over, feeling the smoothness of its wood, every curve and line carved with precision.

The scent of frankincense drew me from my thoughts, its aroma as pungent as ever, even though there was no earthly reason why such a fragrance should be here in my chambers. Did my sister truly linger here? Perhaps our failure to reconcile bothered her as much as it did me. Maybe it kept her here, bound to me, and unable to leave this place like Kia had lingered until her farewell ceremony. That could be why I kept smelling Ishtar's perfume. Maybe her spirit, like Kia's, still walked these hallways. After all, she too suffered a brutal and unexpected death. Maybe she needed encouragement to move on.

But where would she go? To the Great Below, where she would eat dust and clay, and live in eternal darkness, like we Babylonians were raised to expect? Or would it be the Field of Reeds, which was as best I could tell, the Egyptians' perfect ideal of an afterlife, and was all about feasting on good food and lying around under shady trees.

"Ahmose," I started, but found myself unsure how to frame my thoughts, or even whether I wanted to voice them, especially in front of everyone.

Ahmose said nothing, only waited for me to put my thoughts in a logical order.

"Do you think it is possible Ishtar's spirit is still here?" I asked.

"You are thinking of Lady Kia, aren't you?" Merytre looked pointedly at the little lioness. "The things that happened after she went to the West."

"I was never convinced it was really Kia," I said, "but the strange things did stop after her farewell ceremony."

Although Weren thought those events were evidence of magic use, rather than a restless spirit. Maybe that was true. Maybe it wasn't. I didn't know what to believe anymore.

"Has something happened that makes you think Lady Ishtar might be here?" Ettu asked. Her tone was cautious, as if she hadn't yet decided whether my grief had disturbed my mind or I was actually making a valid point.

"I keep smelling frankincense," I admitted. "Every now and then, there's a sudden waft of it, as if she's standing right beside me."

Ettu only shrugged at that and we all looked to Ahmose.

"Her death was very sudden." Ahmose's tone made it clear she took my suggestion seriously. "It was unexpected, and she had much to live for. I suppose it is possible she isn't yet ready to give up on the life she had seen ahead of herself."

"We did previously discuss the possibility of retrieving her body," Ettu said. "Did you want to see if that might be possible so we could bury her properly?"

"But she has already been interred," Sehener said, her face showing her bewilderment. "Shouldn't we leave her body alone so as not to disturb her progression to the afterlife?"

I hesitated, unsure of how to explain without offending her. I hoped Ahmose might intervene, but her eyes were closed and she appeared to be asleep. To my relief, Half offered Sehener an explanation.

"Our beliefs are somewhat different," he said. "Without the correct rites being conducted, a spirit can stay in the mortal world and haunt those it knew."

"The proper funerary rituals ensure the dead move on to the afterlife," Ettu added. "And stay there. Without those rituals, Lady Ishtar might well linger here."

"What if we held a farewell ceremony for her?" Merytre asked. "Like the one for Lady Kia."

"What a wonderful idea." Sehener sounded more eager now. "That way her body won't be disturbed, but you can encourage her spirit to stay in the afterlife, and it might give my lady some measure of comfort."

Ettu only looked at me, waiting. She, at least, had realised I was still sorting through my thoughts.

"If I had known the day I went to her chambers that it would be the last time we spoke…" My voice trailed away.

That discussion hurt to think about. When Ishtar told Pharaoh she carried his child, I had wondered whether she was lying. That perhaps she wanted to gain Pharaoh's approval. Maybe she thought she'd be with child soon enough and he would never know the difference. Maybe it was true and she didn't know until it was too late.

But that day in her chambers, she told me she had lost the babe and she covered her hands with her belly, as if trying to protect the poor thing, even though she knew it was gone, and all I could say was, again?

I had pitied her then, even as I prayed to Marduk that my own child would live. I deeply regretted that our last conversation had been so tense. That I had been so unsympathetic, so suspicious. That I never asked whether she really told Nammu I had demanded she be sent to Egypt with me. I didn't like my memories of my sister being tainted with that suspicion.

They were all watching me, waiting for an answer to Ettu's question.

"No," I said slowly, still piecing my thoughts together. "I wasn't thinking of a farewell ceremony."

As we sailed from Babylon to Egypt, Ahmose told us about how Osiris was murdered and chopped into pieces by his brother. His sister-wife, Isis, used her magic to put him back together again and conceive a son.

If Ishtar's spirit really did linger here, and if we could access her body, could we put the two things back together? Maybe it was a ridiculous idea. Maybe it wasn't even possible. But Ahmose hadn't seemed fazed when I asked for a spell to make me more powerful than Pharaoh. I hesitated, wondering whether I would make a fool of myself if I asked. Perhaps it would be better to wait for a private moment, rather than ask in front of everyone.

"I fear you have some wild idea in mind," Ettu said, her tone dry.

I hesitated, but she shrugged.

"Go on then," she said. "You may as well tell us."

"On the way here," I said to Ahmose, "on the ship, you told us about the murder of Osiris. About how Isis found all his pieces and put him back together."

The look on Ettu's face said she had already guessed where my thought led. Even before I finished, she was shaking her head.

"Surely not," she said. "It would be… blasphemous."

"I don't understand," Sehener said.

"Why?" I asked Ettu. "If the power exists to do such a thing, how can that be wrong? If one can obtain the right spell, why should one not use it?"

"If you want to make such an argument, you may as well say that since Pharaoh has so much power, he should use it as he wishes."

Ettu looked me right in the eyes as she spoke. Her tone was frank and although I bristled at her words, I had to admit she was right. Having power didn't automatically mean one was entitled to use such power.

"It isn't the same," I said, albeit weakly.

"How?" she countered. "Your argument is that if the power exists, it should be used."

"It wouldn't hurt anyone if we were to..." Still, I couldn't make myself say it. It sounded too ludicrous. I wouldn't have even thought such a thing if it wasn't for that tale about Isis and Osiris.

As usual, Ahmose didn't seem startled by my request.

"I did tell you that tale," she said. "But Isis is a goddess. Her knowledge and skills are far beyond anything I could even imagine."

"But it can be done," I pressed.

"In all honesty, I don't know," she said. "But if I had to guess, I would say I don't think it is within the realm of human ability. Not at this point, I'm afraid."

"At this point?" I asked. "What does that mean?"

"Well..." she started. She looked away, over to Ettu, as if asking for her help.

"I think Ahmose is trying to say it has been too long," Ettu said.

"Yes," Ahmose said quickly. "If her death had only just occurred, and we had access to her body immediately, before decay or putrification had time to set in, and we had the right spells, perhaps. But now? We don't know whether her body has been embalmed, but either way, she is no longer in the same state as before. I don't need to know how such a thing might be done to know it is too late to rejoin her spirit with her body."

I understood her reasoning, although it brought to mind images I didn't want to see. What Ishtar might have looked like after Pharaoh was finished with her. Her body naked and still, lying on a workbench in the House of Life, just like Atahar had. And now, her body embalmed, forever stilled into whatever position the embalming priests had decided on. Or not. Left to rot, the flesh decaying from her bones.

I didn't want to imagine her like that. I wanted my memories to be of my joyful sister. The one who danced and sang and exchanged witty banter with eligible men. Even if that hadn't been who she was at the end.

"There is also the matter of duality to consider," Ahmose continued. "Life and death. Light and dark. Good and evil."

"Isis and Nepthys," Merytre offered.

"Two sisters who represent opposites," Ahmose said, with an approving nod in Merytre's direction. "One a goddess of life and the other of death."

"Bastet and Sekhmet," Sehener said. "The protector goddess and the warrior."

Ahmose gave her a nod as well. "Yes, the deities all have their opposites, as does everything in life."

"Like Apsu and Tiamat," Ettu said.

Of course, it would be Ettu who thought of that, she who my sister had named for the goddess, Tiamat. We Babylonians were raised to believe the world began when the sweet waters of Apsu merged with Tiamat's salty waters.

"I don't understand," I said. "What does duality have to do with my sister?"

"Lady Ishtar already traverses the paths of the afterlife," Ahmose said. "If you were to summon her without the proper precautions, there is no way of knowing what consequences might result. If she were to leave the afterlife, does that mean someone else must go there in her place? Or what if you tried to call her, but inadvertently summoned another spirit instead? And what if you cannot return that spirit to the afterlife once you are finished?"

I could only blink at her. I hadn't thought my idea would be easy, but it was clear I hadn't understood the magnitude of what I suggested.

"Are those things possible?" I asked.

Ahmose shrugged. "Who is to say what is possible? Certainly not me. I have never attempted such a thing. But it seems to me there are many ways a spell like that could go wrong."

"What else?" I asked.

"A spirit who is summoned may come unwillingly," she said. "They may seek revenge on the one who called them for dragging them away from the pleasures of the afterlife. Or they may come willingly. Too willingly. It may not be possible to send them back again."

That was exactly what I had hoped for — to restore my sister to life — but the look on Ahmose's face suggested this would not be a desirable thing. My face must have revealed my disappointment, because Ahmose continued.

"It may, however," she said. "Be possible to communicate with a spirit. Briefly, mind," she added quickly at my hopeful expression. "I myself don't have the skill for such a thing, though. You would need someone with far greater magics than I know."

"Where would I find such a person?" I asked.

There was silence in the chamber until Merytre cleared her throat.

"I don't know whether this is true," she said. "But I have heard the Lady Amanitore is something of a sorcerer."

"I, too, have heard rumours about her," Sehener said.

Ahmose nodded "If anyone here in the Palace knows such a spell, I think it would be her."

I blinked at them, caught off guard. Amanitore had been present at Kia's farewell ceremony, although she had taken no greater part in the ceremony than I had. I had spoken with her once or twice since then. She had never been particularly friendly and I couldn't imagine she would want to help me with such a thing.

"Tell me what you know about her." I directed my words to the chamber at large, unsure who would know the most.

"She is Nubian," Merytre offered.

"Like Abar," I said.

Only Abar called herself a Kushite. Nubian, as best I could tell, was a derogatory term, indicative of how poorly the Egyptians viewed the foreigners. One of my maids had referred to Abar as being an upside-down person, which seemed to mean she was believed to consume what would normally be expelled from the body.

"I have heard she sometimes knows things she shouldn't," Sehener said.

"Like what?" I asked.

Sehener frowned as she thought.

"I can't remember a specific example," she said finally. "Just that she knows things nobody else does."

"She has born Pharaoh two sons," Merytre said. "And apparently she has only been with him twice."

"Oh, yes," Sehener said. "I heard she used a spell to get herself with child so quickly."

I carefully avoided looking at Ahmose. Such a spell was not all that rare, as both she and I knew.

"I heard another Ornament from Nubia said she was well known as a sorceress there," Merytre said. "You might remember her, Sehener. Maletasen, I think her name was."

"I know who you mean," Sehener said, "although I never met her. I think she went to the West shortly after I started working here."

Did Abar know about Amanitore? Had her reputation in Kush been such that even my reluctant maid knew her?

"What else?" I asked.

Sehener and Merytre studied each other, each apparently waiting for the other to respond, and it seemed neither knew anything else. So perhaps Amanitore wasn't a sorcerer after all. She might merely have made a couple of lucky guesses about things people would prefer to keep secret. Or she might be like Ahmose, someone with a modest amount of arcane knowledge. Such a woman was always assumed to know more than she did.

"I will speak with Amanitore," I said.

"You will do as you will," Ahmose said. "I only pray to Amun that you consider it carefully."

CHAPTER 35

The following morning, Sehener and Merytre went to ask Amanitore if I could speak with her. I didn't know her well enough to go to her chambers uninvited. They returned with word that she would be walking in the grounds at noon. I wondered at her choice of location. Surely her chambers would provide a more private location for our discussion?

But as Sehener and I made our way through the Palace shortly before noon, I realised it was actually a clever suggestion. If we met in the grounds, it would look like we happened on each other by chance, and it would raise no suspicions about what reason we had to meet in secret.

"Oh, is that Lady Hilde?" Sehener asked as we reached the ground floor. "She seems quite lovely and you have not spoken with her for some time."

Not since the day I encountered her in the gardens and discovered she had already experienced Pharaoh's brutality. She was angry I didn't warn her. Since then, I had seen no more of her than a glimpse from afar.

Hilde's body seemed to stiffen when she saw me and I expected her to immediately turn in a different direction. But her maid — her cousin — said something to her and they came straight towards me.

"Kassaya." Hilde gave me a nod as she halted in front of me.

"Hilde." My tone was warmer than hers. I couldn't help myself from looking at her throat, searching for evidence she had suffered again at Pharaoh's hands. Her skin was unmarked. Of course, she noticed my gaze.

"He has not called for me again," she said coolly.

I had failed to warn her. I would never make that mistake again.

"If he does, there is something you must know," I said very quietly. I glanced around to make sure nobody but our own maids would hear. "You must not fight him. If he puts his hands on you, you must let him do whatever he wants. That is how you save yourself."

Hilde backed away. Her gaze was even colder now and she gave me a disgusted look.

"I cannot believe you would suggest such a thing," she said. "Not after what you told me about your sister."

She turned and strode away.

"Good day to you," she called over her shoulder. "I don't expect we shall have much to say to each other in future."

Her maid gave me a scathing look, then hurried to catch up with her.

It was no more than I deserved. I could hardly have expected Hilde to be pleased at learning I withheld something of such magnitude from her. Especially, as she pointed out, since I had told her my sister was murdered. I never said Pharaoh was responsible, but she had obviously guessed.

Sehener was busy studying the floor. Ettu would have had something to say, but Sehener was still more reserved in her opinions. As a good lady's maid should be, I supposed. She didn't speak until we were outside.

"Lady Amanitore said she would be over that way," she said with a nod.

We strolled along the path, our leisurely pace hopefully suggesting we had no particular destination in mind. Only a few minutes passed before I spotted a familiar figure ahead of us.

"There she is," I said to Sehener, although the comment was unnecessary as she could surely see Amanitore as well.

As we approached, Sehener dropped back behind me. Amanitore was accompanied by two maids, who already walked some distance behind her. We stopped in front of each other and she acknowledged me with a brief nod.

"Kassaya," she said.

"Amanitore. Thank you for meeting with me."

She turned and started back the way she had come, moving further away from the Palace and the guards who waited at the front doors. Her legs were longer than mine and I had to hurry to keep up with her.

"I assume there is a reason for your request," she said after a few moments of silence.

"There is. I have heard you have a reputation as a sorcerer."

"Is that so?" Her voice was casual and she continued to stare straight ahead. "Folk will say as they choose and there is little one can do about it."

"So it is not true?" My fragile hope deflated.

"I said only I can't help what folk say about me."

Already, I sensed this would be a frustrating conversation. If Amanitore intended to be obscure about what she said, I would never find out if she could do what I wanted. I would have to speak plainly.

"Do you know a spell that would allow me to communicate with my sister?" I asked.

She shot me a sideways glance. I had surprised her, it seemed.

"The one who disappeared?" she asked.

"The one who was murdered."

We walked in silence for a few paces.

"Perhaps," she said.

I waited, but she offered nothing further.

"Would you be willing to help me?" I asked.

If I hadn't been looking at her, I would have missed the odd way she waggled her head, a response that seemed to be something between a yes and a no.

"What do you propose to do for me in return?" she asked.

"I have jewels," I said quickly. "I will give you whatever you want if you can facilitate a conversation with my sister."

"I have plenty of jewels," she said. "And no need for any more. I will take a favour. A favour of my choosing at the time of my choice."

I barely hesitated. It wasn't a good deal for me, I knew that. It was too broad and Marduk only knew what manner of favour she might ask, but now the possibility of speaking with Ishtar dangled in front of me, I knew I would give anything in the world for that chance.

"I accept," I said. "A favour of your choice."

She stopped walking and turned to examine me with a seriousness that took me aback. I waited silently, unsure whether she had yet decided if she would help me.

"Two days," she said. "Be in the chapel at sunset. Bring something that belonged to your sister and also an offering for her."

Then she turned in the direction she had originally come from and strode off. Her maids hurried after her. I watched her until she passed behind a tree and was lost to my sight.

CHAPTER 36

That evening, I went looking for Khaemmalu. Maybe he wouldn't want to talk to me, let alone anything more, but I couldn't give up on him that easily. I might have expected he would leave me wandering the grounds for hours, but he revealed himself almost as soon as I left the torch-lit path.

"Back here," he said.

I followed his voice into the shadows. His hand found mine and I relaxed a little. He wouldn't touch me if he hated me now. Or, at least, I didn't think he would.

He stopped and turned to face me. I took a breath, ready to apologise until I ran out of words if it meant he would forgive me.

"Don't," he said. "I don't need to hear your reasons, or your excuses, or your apologies. I was angry, yes. Very angry. At first, I wasn't sure I could forgive you. But once I calmed down, I realised something."

He paused and I discovered I was holding my breath. I let it out in a rush. Whatever his realisation, it wasn't that he hated me.

"I realised all that matters is that we are together." His fingers found my hand again, twining through mine. I clung to him.

"Kassaya, I have suggested before that you should leave, but I don't think you took me seriously, so I'm going to say it again. It is more important than ever now. If you have any intention of leaving, you must do it before the babe is born. I will come with you. We can go anywhere you want. I have a lot of training, many skills. I will find work wherever we go, and I will look after you. Both of you."

Tears welled, and for just a moment, I considered it. I really did.

"I can't," I said. "I wish I could, but if I leave, the alliance will be broken, and that could mean war for Babylon. At the least, it would mean the cancellation of trade deals, which could be disastrous for my country. I can't let my father down, and I won't be responsible for the consequences."

"But this was never your choice, was it? You wouldn't have come here if it was up to you."

"No, I wouldn't have. But that doesn't matter. From the time I could understand it, I knew my fate would be chosen for me. I accepted that."

I wanted to say it wasn't as bad as it could be, but that would be a lie. The man my father had given me to was the worst sort, and my situation here was precarious, to say the least. I hadn't done a very good job of making Pharaoh happy. He would be pleased when I delivered him a son, though, even though he'd made it perfectly clear my child wouldn't ever be his heir. And there was my plan to expose him. To prevent any other woman from suffering at his hands. How could I leave before I saw that through?

"Kassaya?"

Khaemmalu's voice brought me back to the present.

"I'm sorry, did you say something?" I asked.

"I lost you for a few moments there," he said. "I was saying I worry about the danger to you here, especially given your contact with Pharaoh. Those Ornaments who never interact with him are probably safe enough, but you have met him too many times. He asks for you. I fear that could make you a target. The danger here is too great."

For a moment, I considered telling him about my plan. That I only needed to keep myself safe for a while longer, because eventually Ahmose would obtain the right spell, and we would expose Pharaoh, and put a stop to his crimes, and even if I somehow failed, there was still Tiye's plan. But I couldn't tell him. The more he knew, the greater the risk to him.

"I can't leave," I said. "I'm sorry, Khaemmalu, but I can't."

"If you won't do it for yourself, think of your babe," he said.

His words hit me hard, as he surely knew they would. If my plan went awry, what would happen to my son? If I was uncovered, would they let him be born before they carried out my sentence? Maybe I should wait until after his birth. Surely his status as a son of Pharaoh would protect him, even if being his mother couldn't protect me.

"I can't," I said at last. "Please stop asking me."

Shortly before sunset on the day Amanitore had indicated, I set off for the chapel. Ettu, Merytre and Sehener all wanted to accompany me, but someone needed to stay since Ahmose was so unwell. After much discussion, they agreed it would be Sehener and she didn't look as disappointed as I might have expected.

As we descended the last flight of stairs, I spotted Amankhau's back disappearing down a hallway, and breathed a sigh of relief. Other than our brief conversation the day he introduced me to Weren, I hadn't spoken to him since he saw us smuggling Half inside. Even though I no longer waited for a summons to present myself to Pharaoh to account for making him so angry, every knock could still be one of the administrators, come to inspect my chambers and find the mystery person Amankhau saw.

Outside, the air was blessedly cool. The long-promised change of season must have finally arrived. As we walked the length of the Palace and around to the little chapel where we held Kia's farewell ceremony, I tried to tell myself not to hope for too much. Maybe Amanitore wasn't as much of a sorcerer as folk said. Maybe she wouldn't be able to contact Ishtar, or Ishtar wouldn't want to talk to me. It was better to go without expectations, and then at least I wouldn't be disappointed.

Ettu and Merytre made no attempt at conversation, for which I was grateful. We were halfway to the chapel when my belly tightened and spasmed. I winced and put my hand over it.

"Are you well?" Ettu asked quickly. "Do you need to sit down?"

"Should I call a guard to help you?" Merytre asked.

"No, no." The feeling had been strong and left me winded. "Perhaps we could just walk a little slower."

"You can take my arm and lean on me if you need to," Merytre said.

"Is the babe kicking?" Ettu asked.

"I'm not sure." I slowed my pace, keeping my hand on my belly. The babe seemed to be still, sleeping perhaps. "It didn't feel like him kicking."

"It is too early for him to be born, isn't it?" she asked.

"Not for another couple of months yet," I said.

"Maybe you were just walking too fast," she said in the decided tone she used when she had made up her mind about something. "It is nothing to be concerned about."

Still, I didn't miss the sideways glances she darted at me when she thought I wasn't looking. She was more worried than she had let on and that made me worried. What did she know that I didn't? The physician said everything was progressing as it should be. It had been around a week since he last examined me, so he would probably come again soon. For the first time, I'd actually be pleased to see him.

The sun was close to setting as the chapel came into view, casting the sky in a brilliant shade of orange.

"Should we wait over there?" Merytre asked Ettu, pointing to a grassy patch beside a flower bed. "That looks like a most pleasant spot."

"Actually," Ettu said. "I was hoping my lady wouldn't mind if I listen in?"

"Of course not." After all, Ettu had served Ishtar long before she became my maid. "Merytre, you may come in too, or wait out here, as you prefer."

"If it is all the same to you, I will wait here," Merytre said. "I never knew Lady Ishtar well, so it wouldn't be right for me to attend."

We left her settling herself on the grass. As Ettu and I reached the chapel's open door, I hesitated, unsure whether to go in or wait to be invited.

"Don't just stand there," came Amanitore's voice.

The chapel's interior was lit with candles, dozens of them set out on the floor. I walked carefully, mindful of how easy it would be for my hem to sweep across a flame and burn the building down.

Amanitore waited in the centre of the candles. Beside her on the floor stood a large cauldron and a basket. A sweet-smelling smoke drifted up from the cauldron's fire, tickling my nose. I breathed through my mouth and hoped I wouldn't sniffle all the way through the ceremony.

"Do you intend to come in or go back out?" Amanitore asked.

Surprised, I looked at her, but realised she meant Ettu.

"Oh, I can stay here," Ettu said. "I don't want to get in the way."

"You will either participate or leave." Amanitore eyed her cooly. "Make your choice."

Ettu looked to me, clearly unsure about how to respond.

"Come in," I said to her. "You said you wanted to be here."

"Oh, but—" she started, but stopped at Amanitore's huff. She made her way through the candles and came to stand beside me.

"It is a narcissus, isn't it?" she asked, gesturing to the floor. "The candles."

Now she had said it, I didn't know how I missed seeing the

pattern earlier. The candles were indeed laid out around us in a way that suggested the five petals of a narcissus.

"You may stand there," Amanitore said to me. I moved to the spot she pointed at. "And you there," to Ettu.

That meant the three of us were arranged at equal points around the cauldron, which stood in the flower's centre.

"Did you bring something that belonged to your sister?" Amanitore asked me.

I fumbled in my pouch and retrieved the jewelled hair pins I had taken from her chambers when I searched them for any evidence that might reveal her fate. I held them out to Amanitore, but she gestured towards the cauldron.

"Throw them in?" I asked.

She nodded and I tossed the hair pins into the flames.

Amanitore stooped to pluck something from her basket. She cast it into the fire before I could see it. A pungent aroma rose. She held out her hands to Ettu and I, and as I took her hand, I found mine trembled just the tiniest bit. In my other hand, Ettu's palm was damp. It reassured me to know she, too, was nervous.

Amanitore closed her eyes and seemed to sway a little from side to side. Ettu and I exchanged nervous glances. I wasn't sure whether we were supposed to do the same. Before I could decide, Amanitore started humming. It was a slow, monotonous tune, only three or four notes which repeated in various combinations.

As I listened, a deep feeling of stillness settled over me. I found myself standing with my eyes closed and after a while, I could hardly remember ever having done anything else. I had been standing here forever, my hands joined with Ettu and Amanitore, listening to the sound of Amanitore's peculiar song and the crackle of the fire, and smelling the strange aroma from whatever she had tossed in the flames.

At some point, the smell changed. Now it was the unmistakable scent of frankincense. As if she knew I was about to look, Amanitore spoke.

"Keep your eyes closed," she said. "Regardless of what happens, you must not look. I will look for you. I will keep you safe."

I nodded, unsure whether I was supposed to speak. It felt like something that might not be permitted.

"Ishtar," Amanitore said. "Daughter of Marduk-apla-iddina of Babylon, sister of Kassaya, Princess of Babylon. We bid you come forth to speak with us, but this invitation is temporary. You must return to whence you came once our conversation is concluded."

"I accept," came Ishtar's voice.

I was so startled, I almost opened my eyes, but remembered Amanitore's warning just in time. Her voice was faint and thready, but it was unmistakably my sister.

"Kassaya," Amanitore said. "The pathway is open. Speak, but be swift. I may not be able to hold it open for long."

I had spent the last two days rehearsing what I wanted to say to Ishtar, but my careful words fled and I couldn't think of a single thing to say.

"Sister," Ishtar said. "Is that you? I feel your presence, although I don't see you."

"Ishtar." Tears welled, but I kept my eyes firmly closed. "Are you… are you well where you are?"

"You need not fret for me, sister," she said. "But you, are you safe?"

"I am safe enough." How much did Amanitore know about the missing women? I wasn't sure what I could say in front of her. "Ishtar, I am sorry for what I said that last time we spoke. About your babe."

"Aah." Her voice was soft, not much more than a sigh. "My babe. I had forgotten. I was supposed to be a mother."

"You would have if you hadn't gotten sick."

It wasn't important anymore whether Ishtar actually knew she was with child when she told Pharaoh she was. It was a petty thing for me to focus on.

"You abandoned me," she said. "In the time I needed you the most. I had forgotten that as well."

What else had she forgotten? Perhaps it was wrong of me to summon her like this. To remind her of things she had already let go of. Her afterlife would be easier without the pain of such memories. I should tell Amanitore to release her. Let Ishtar return to her rest. I shouldn't have disturbed her. But I couldn't let her go without saying what I came here for.

"I'm sorry," I said. "I have regretted that conversation ever since, and I regret that I never apologised to you."

"It matters not now," she said.

Her voice was a little fainter. Was the channel already closing? I would never speak with my sister again and I suddenly knew the thing I would regret not saying.

"Ishtar, you used me," I said, "in your plan to avoid being sent to Egypt. I resented you for that. Maybe I even hated you a little. It was wrong of you to have me sent in your place."

"Yes." Her voice came stronger now. "I remember. I used you. I was sorry to do it, but I had no other choice."

She did have a choice, though. She could have done as our father told her to and come to Egypt.

"Did you tell Nammu I asked for her to be sent here with me?" I asked.

"Nammu." Ishtar was silent and I thought she was gone. I regretted wasting my last moments with her on Nammu, but then she spoke. "I don't think so. Maybe I did. I can't remember."

"They buried you as a queen," I said. "I know you would like that."

I wouldn't tell her she hadn't received the proper rites according to either of the cultures we straddled. She didn't need to know such a thing.

"A queen." Ishtar's voice sounded as if she smiled. "I always knew I would be a queen. I was born for that."

"You were." The tears spilled down my cheeks, but still I didn't let myself open my eyes.

"I remember what happened to me," she said, her voice surprised. "How he hurt me."

"I'm sorry. I should have warned you before you went."

"I probably wasn't the first. And I won't be the last."

I tried to find a response, but my throat choked and I couldn't speak.

"One day, someone will stop him," Ishtar said. "One day, someone will be brave enough to stand up to him."

"Make your farewells," Amanitore said. "You have only another few moments."

"Ishtar, I love you." The words burst out of me, urgent with the knowledge that this was the last thing I would ever say to my sister. "I'm sorry I didn't treat you better once you came to Egypt, but I was very glad to have you here with me."

"Sister," came her sigh. "Sister."

Silence.

Amanitore released my hand. The flames crackled as she tossed something else onto them. The frankincense faded, replaced again with the pungent aroma I had smelled previously.

"You may open your eyes," Amanitore said. She gestured towards the cauldron. "Your offering."

I retrieved the shell from my pouch. It was a delicate thing, creamy in colour, and brought by my Father from Syria when I was a child. He had brought one for Ishtar, too, but she favoured mine over hers. For weeks, she begged me to trade with her and it was one of the few times in our childhood that Ishtar didn't get what she wanted. I touched the shell to my lips, then tossed it into the fire.

"Farewell, Sister," I said.

CHAPTER 38

As Ettu and I emerged from the chapel, Merytre scrambled to her feet, her face eager. She opened her mouth to say something, but seemed to stop at a look from Ettu. We didn't speak at all on the way back to my chambers, and for once, I was thankful not to encounter Khaemmalu. There was no room in my head for him tonight.

The conversation with Ishtar had left me conflicted. On one hand, there was some measure of relief at having said the things I regretted not saying earlier. On the other, though, the conversation hadn't been entirely satisfactory. I had no resolution as to why she used me the way she did, or whether she really lied to Nammu. I wasn't even entirely certain she had been with child when she said she was.

It was her comment about stopping Pharaoh that haunted me now and it strengthened my resolve to expose him. *One day, someone will stop him,* she said. *One day, someone will be brave enough to stand up to him.* I wanted that to be me. For the sake of my sister. For the sake of every other woman he had killed, and every woman he would kill, because nobody was brave enough to expose him.

Back in my chambers, I stopped only long enough to snatch up a slice of bread. I didn't want to deal with questions about the ceremony, or how I felt about it. It had left me so weary that I ate, then went straight to sleep.

The following morning, I felt dazed and a little odd, as if I wasn't fully in my own body. Sitting on the stool in my bathing chamber, I barely noticed my maids. Later, when I sat in my bedchamber while they continued attending to me, I drifted in and out of a dream-like state. Perhaps I was just particularly tired today, or perhaps it was some after-effect from yesterday's ceremony. Surely, Amanitore would have warned me if I should expect to feel strange, though.

I caught Abar's eye at one point. She stood by the door of my bedchamber, glaring at me just as fiercely as she had ever since I told her Atahar was believed to be dead. Could Amanitore help Abar speak with her sister too? Maybe Abar would stop hating me if I could arrange that.

Although the conversation with Ishtar had not resolved all the questions I had hoped it would, it did give me some measure of peace, and maybe Ishtar would stay in the afterlife now she, too, had said what she needed to. *One day, someone will stop him. One day, someone will be brave enough to stand up to him.* Was that why she had lingered here? She wanted to tell me that someone needed to stop Pharaoh?

Later that morning, Panouk came knocking and asked to speak with me privately. I went out to the hallway so as not to disturb Ahmose who was dozing in her chair.

Panouk cleared his throat and gave me a look that suggested he felt uncomfortable about whatever he had come to say.

"I do hope you aren't here to tell me Weren wants to interview Ahmose again," I said.

It was either that, or Weren was ready to interview me.

"Not exactly," he said and cleared his throat again.

I waited, a little bemused by his apparent discomfort. I had never seen the administrator look so ill at ease before.

"Weren has revealed to me that he has, uh—" again, he cleared his throat "—new information that pertains to his interview with Ahmose. I wanted to discuss this with you in private, given you asked Ahmose be excused from further interviews. I am sure there is a perfectly reasonable explanation for what he has learned."

He stopped and I nodded for him to continue.

"Lady Tiye's maid, Henuttawy, is known to be a woman of some herbal knowledge and we are aware that she, at times, uh, supplies herbs to other residents."

My heart felt like it stilled, then resumed its beating at double time. No, surely not. What daughter would betray her own mother?

"Weren's interview with her revealed she was supplying Ahmose with a certain herb." He studied me as he spoke and I was careful to keep my face blank. "A herb which has no known medical properties. As I'm sure you can appreciate, this is rather sensitive information and I wanted to bring it to your attention straight away."

Why hadn't I thought to prepare an explanation for this? But, of course, I never expected Henuttawy to reveal such a thing. My previous discussion with Panouk had left me quite certain he could be trusted. The decision I had to make now was whether to rely on that instinct, or to lie and pray to Marduk he believed me.

"I hope you know," he continued, "I am here to help you. If there is something you need to tell me, this is the time to do it."

He didn't say, if there was something I needed to tell Weren. He didn't say, if there was something I needed to confess. His choice of words could hardly be anything other than deliberate.

"Why would Henuttawy tell Weren such a thing?" I asked. "Even if it is true, what benefit is there to her to tell him?"

"There are, of course, certain agreements made when Weren conducts such an interview."

Panouk gave me an expectant look, as if he thought I knew what he meant. I shrugged at him.

"The interviewees are promised a reward," he said. "If they can provide new evidence that aids the investigation."

Henuttawy exposed Ahmose for a reward. So much for Ahmose's belief her daughter could be trusted. And it raised yet another question. Why didn't Ahmose tell us she had been offered such a reward? Was it because she did, in fact, intend to give Weren enough information to receive some payment from him?

"I am aware that Henuttawy has on occasion supplied Ahmose with such a herb." There was no point in denying it. "But I must ask you to trust me when I say I can't tell you what it was used for. I can only assure you Ahmose no longer has any of that herb in her possession and does not have any intention of seeking more of it."

He searched my face, perhaps looking for evidence of duplicity. I looked him right in the eyes and prayed he would feel the truth of my words. He was surely clever enough to realise that I, like he, spoke carefully. At length, he nodded.

"Thank you for your honesty," he said.

"What will you tell Weren?"

"That I have discussed the matter with you directly and have no further concerns."

I let out the breath I hadn't realised I was holding. I had been right to trust him. Perhaps this might be a moment in which he would be more receptive to hearing what I had tried to tell him previously.

"Panouk, there is something I need to bring to your attention now," I said.

He nodded.

"It is about Amankhau."

I waited for his reaction, but again, he only nodded.

"I believe he is involved in covering up the disappearance of certain women," I said.

I didn't yet have the courage to tell him who Amankhau was aiding in doing such a thing. Panouk finally broke our gaze and looked down at the floor.

"I share your suspicion," he said. "I have suspected it for some time. There are certain… circumstances that led me to believe a connection."

"Is there nothing you can do about it? Can't you remove him from the Palace? We would be much safer without him."

"I don't have the authority to do such a thing. He was appointed by Pharaoh and only Pharaoh can remove him. As I'm sure you can appreciate, I can hardly go to Pharaoh with such an accusation."

He looked me right in the eyes and I suspected his words were intended to hint he knew the bigger truth.

"But you, in particular, must be very careful with Amankhau," he said. "He came to me a couple of days ago, claiming he saw you and your maid with what he described as a suspicious person whose identity was concealed. He wanted me to authorise him to search your chambers."

"And what did you tell him?" I could hardly breathe as I waited for his reply.

"He happened to mention you said he imagined it. That perhaps the heat had been too fierce for him that day, and you sent a healer to tend to him. I convinced him the heat had indeed been particularly bad and it was well known that it can cause hallucinations."

I let out my breath in a rush.

"I suggested he take some time off," Panouk continued. "That he has been working far too hard and should have a short holiday. He agreed. We won't see him for a few days."

"Thank you, Panouk." My voice had probably never been so

sincere in speaking with the administrator and I hoped he could feel my genuine appreciation.

He gave me a stiff nod, but I noted a slight blush to his cheeks.

"I'm sure it hardy needs to be said," he added, "but you must be entirely above reproach from now on. You and all your servants."

CHAPTER 39

In a mood of reconciliation after my conversation with Panouk, I decided to visit Tiye. We hadn't spoken since the day we discussed how long she had known Ahmose was Henuttawy's mother. My anger at that discovery had faded somewhat. After all, we had only just met when she found out and she didn't know whether she could trust me. But there had been plenty of opportunities since then for her to tell me, and she had kept the information to herself, as if it was a game piece she had not yet decided to put into play.

I wanted to put that disappointment behind me, though. Losing Ishtar had taught me it was better not to harbour resentment against someone for what they did or didn't do. This place was my home now, whether I liked it or not, and Tiye was an influential woman. We each had our plans to expose Pharaoh, and even though I had no intention of working with her, we at least had the same aim.

As I knocked, I braced myself. Surely this time it would be Henuttawy who opened the door. She undoubtedly knew I knew, and I hadn't yet decided whether I should say anything. I would wait to see how she reacted when she saw me. But it was

214

Bennerib who let me in, and neither Henuttawy nor Nammu were in the sitting chamber.

"Kassaya." Tiye's voice was as warm as it ever was as she left the window and went the couches. She nodded towards the couch opposite her as she sat down, an unusually polite invitation for her. Perhaps it was her way of apologising.

"I hear Weren is still conducting his interviews." Her tone was conversational now, as if she had no knowledge that those interviews included one of my own servants. "It would seem, however, he hasn't found what he was looking for."

If she knew Henuttawy had been supplying Ahmose with that particular herb, or that Henuttawy had received a reward for telling Weren, she gave no sign of it.

"It sounds like his interviews were a waste of time then," I said, determined to give nothing away. "And caused much distress for those he interviewed."

"I heard about your servant collapsing. Has she recovered?"

Her query surprised me. I would never expect Tiye to ask after the health of a mere servant. But then, my servant was her servant's mother. Perhaps that gave her a reason to care, at least a little.

"She has some tonics from the healer," I said, "although she is being rather stubborn about not taking them, so I suppose she is as well as can be expected in the circumstances."

Tiye smoothed her skirt, then stretched her arm along the back of the couch. Clearly, it was my turn to make conversation.

"I had an interesting conversation with Panouk this morning," I said.

"Oh?" She raised one eyebrow at me. "Do tell."

I relayed our conversation about Amankhau, but kept the details about Henuttawy's betrayal to myself. As long as Tiye continued to keep secrets from me, I would do the same.

"Hmm," she said when I finished.

Her non-committal reply irked me.

"I think we can trust him," I said.

"We?" She gave me a cool look.

"We both want the same thing."

"Does that mean you have changed your mind?" she asked. "You will join with us?"

I could hardly tell her I had my own plan. She would likely see it as a betrayal, or a competition, and the work I had just done to smooth things over between us would be wasted.

"I don't want to be involved with selecting a replacement for Pharaoh," I said. "I don't know anything about your son, other than what you have told me."

Her eyes narrowed. I had said the wrong thing.

"My son is a good man," she said. "He is intelligent and well educated. He is also compassionate, and given the chance, I believe he will be a wise ruler. That sloth, Ramses, is nothing compared to my Pentaweret."

"I wasn't suggesting otherwise," I said quickly, "but I don't think it should be up to us to make such a decision. Surely there are rules about the progression."

"Pharaoh's will is what determines the progression, and he is not fit to make such a decision. My son will be the next pharaoh. You can work with us, and benefit from that alliance later, or you can work against us." She gave me a shrug. "Your choice."

"I'm not working against you," I said. "I just don't want to be involved. It is not the same thing."

"It seems simple to me," she said. "But you will make your own choice."

She changed the topic then and spoke of inconsequential matters until I rose to leave. Then her voice changed.

"Before you go," she said.

I quickly sat back down. Something told me this wouldn't be news I would like.

"Henuttawy has left my service," she said, rather tersely.

"She has left?"

"That is what I just said." Her voice was irritable now.

"Whose service has she transferred to?"

"Nobody's."

I waited, but she only looked at me, apparently expecting me to understand. I shrugged and she gave a heavy sigh, as if I was too stupid to tolerate.

"She has left the Palace," she said.

Still, I couldn't quite comprehend what she meant.

"Left?"

She nodded.

"When?" I asked.

"Yesterday."

Ahmose was in my chambers this morning. They hadn't left together. Had Henuttawy had fled and left her mother behind?

Then it hit me. Ishtar's gem. The one that was promised to Messui. Henuttawy had it.

"Are you sure she left?" I asked. "After all—"

"Yes, Kassaya, I am well aware that women tend to disappear from here, and yes, I am certain. I sent Benerib to check her bed in the maids' dormitory. Her things are gone."

"She left nothing behind?"

Maybe she returned the gem to Ahmose before she left. I clung to the thought. Yes, that's exactly what happened. She had to leave, for some reason that was unknown to us, so she returned the gem to her mother and made her farewells. Ahmose was obviously too distraught to tell us yet.

"Everything she owned is gone," Tiye said. "What surprises me is that she doesn't seem to have taken anything of mine. Usually, in a case like this, when a maid runs off without notice, she secrets away a few jewels to fund her new life. Henuttawy took nothing that was not her own, as far as I can tell."

But then, Henuttawy didn't need to steal anything of Tiye's. She already had Ishtar's gem and she had her reward from Weren. It seemed Tiye didn't know that.

As I returned to my chambers, my mind raced. It seemed unrealistic to hope Henuttawy had indeed returned Ishtar's gem. A woman who intended to flee and make a new life for herself, and who was in possession of a treasure that would let her make that life anything she wanted it to be, would hardly give it up.

Back in my chambers, I hesitated to ask Ahmose what I needed to. I didn't want to sound like I accused her of doing something underhanded in not telling me Henuttawy had returned the gem.

It was Sehener who resolved the dilemma for me.

"I heard some news while my lady was with Lady Tiye." Her voice was cautious, but that wasn't unusual for Sehener, who always tried not to offend anyone.

"Good gossip?" Merytre asked cheerily, her hands busy with her needlework.

"Not exactly." Sehener shot Ahmose a look and I suddenly realised what her news was. "Ahmose, have you spoken with Henuttawy today?"

"I haven't seen her for a couple of days," Ahmose said. She was resting her head on the back of the chair with her eyes closed, but she opened them now to squint at Sehener. "Why do you ask?"

"Well." Sehener seemed to squirm and looked decidedly uncomfortable, which apparently made Ahmose realise her news might be important.

The old woman sat up straighter and peered more intently at Sehener.

"What is it?" she asked. "Is she ill?"

"I heard she has left," Sehener said in a very quiet voice.

"What's that?" Ahmose asked. "Speak up, dear. I can't hear you when you mumble like that."

Sehener repeated her words and Ahmose gave her a blank look.

"Left?" she asked. "What does that mean?"

"She is gone," Sehener said.

Ahmose shook her head.

"It is true," I said. "Tiye told me. Apparently Henuttawy took all her things and left the Palace yesterday."

"She has left," Ahmose repeated dully. Her gaze rose to meet mine. "And she took everything?"

I nodded, knowing what she really asked. Did Henuttawy take the gem.

Ahmose's face went a rather odd shade and she seemed to gasp for breath. She raised her hand to clutch her chest.

"Ahmose?" I dashed over to her, but then didn't know what to do.

"I will send for the healer." Merytre was already on her way to the door.

"I trusted her," Ahmose said.

She gave a strangled groan, then she collapsed.

The others rushed to my side as I tried to stop Ahmose from falling off the chair.

"Is she…" Sehener asked.

Ahmose made a sound like a wheeze.

"Oh, she is alive," Ettu said. "I thought—"

She stopped as Ahmose's eyes closed and her body slumped.

"Help me lie her on the floor," I said.

I didn't know why I thought that might help. Tall lifted Ahmose from her chair and gently lay her down.

"Go," Sehener said to him. "The healer will be here in a moment."

The two men fled down the hallway to their bedchamber.

"I don't think she is breathing," Ettu said.

"Oh, Ahmose." Sehener wiped away tears.

I stared down at the old woman, too shocked to know what to do or say. We stayed frozen like that until the healer arrived. It was the same one who had attended her last time.

"Make some space please," she said crisply. "You can all go and sit down."

We stood back and she didn't ask again. She set her fingers against Ahmose's chest, then on her wrist, and leaned down to listen to her breath.

"I'm sorry," she said. "There is nothing I can do. She has already gone to the West."

"She is dead?" I asked, feeling rather stupid. But I wanted to be very certain I hadn't misunderstood.

"I'm afraid so," the healer said.

"Are you sure there is nothing you can do?" I asked.

Her face was sympathetic.

"I'm sorry," she said. "Ahmose knew her time was coming to an end. I'm afraid her heart has failed."

She got to her feet.

"I will advise Panouk and he will make the appropriate arrangements. Somebody will come to collect her shortly, so this is the time for you to say your goodbyes."

She went to the door, but hesitated, turning back as if she intended to say something else. Whatever she saw on our faces must have changed her mind, though, because she left without another word.

Sehener started to say something, but choked on a sob. Merytre put an arm around her and together they cried.

"I suppose I had better go lock the men's door," Ettu said. "Before anyone else arrives."

She disappeared down the hallway and I heard the door to the men's bedchamber open and close.

I stared down at Ahmose. My mind was blank and my eyes dry. I couldn't quite believe what had happened. Surely there was some mistake. The healer must be wrong. I didn't notice Ettu come to stand beside me until she spoke.

"It must have been the shock," she said. "It was too much for her."

"Oh, it's all my fault," Sehener said with a wail. "I shouldn't have told her."

I shook my head, still unable to find any words.

"Perhaps you should sit down," Ettu said. "You look quite pale."

I heard her, but didn't comprehend she meant me until she took my arm. She led me back to the couch.

"But she was just…" I waved my hands, unsure what I was trying to express.

"She was a very old woman," Ettu said, "with a bad heart. I am grateful to have met her. She had a lot of wisdom and I learned much from her."

She turned her attention to Sehener and Merytre. I marvelled at Ettu's ability to keep her composure even in such a grim situation. But then, she didn't know just how dire things really were. None of them did.

They didn't know Henuttawy had absconded with the gem that was meant to pay for a spell to make me powerful enough to hold Pharaoh responsible for his crimes. And they didn't know she was also my only means of contacting Messui, who was probably still searching Pharaoh's library for more spells for me.

That was it. The complete and utter failure of my plan.

CHAPTER 40

$\mathcal{P}$anouk arrived promptly, followed by two men and a runner boy.

"My lady," he said. "I am very sorry to hear this news."

I accepted his words with a nod. There was nothing to say, after all. Ahmose was dead and my plan was in tatters. Unless Tiye's plan came to fruition, Pharaoh would be free to continue with his murderous ways.

Panouk directed the two men, who wrapped Ahmose's body in a length of linen and lifted her. They carried her out of my chambers with remarkable speed. Panouk gestured towards the runner, who waited at the door, his curious gaze taking in my chambers. He was much younger than the runners usually were. Perhaps he was new.

"Is there anyone who needs to be advised?" Panouk asked. "The boy here is at your disposal should you need to send word of Ahmose's departure for the West."

I blinked at him and it took me a little too long to find a reply.

"No, I... There is nobody who needs to be advised."

After all, we had no idea where Henuttawy was. She was Ahmose's only living relative, as far as I knew.

"Family?" Panouk prodded. "Friends?"

I cast a glance at Ettu, who quickly stepped forward.

"I believe everyone who mattered to Ahmose is already here," she said. "There is nobody else who needs to be advised."

"Well, then." Panouk cleared his throat. "I shall leave you to mourn in private. Should there be anything you need, anything at all, send for me and I will come as quickly as I can."

"Thank you," I managed.

He left, shooing the runner ahead of him. The door closed and Ettu, who seemed to be the only one of us with any presence of mind, barred it behind him, then went to let the men out.

We took our usual places and sat in silence. I tried not to look at Ahmose's empty chair.

"At least she got to know Henuttawy before—" Sehener stopped as a sob burst out instead of whatever she had meant to say.

Tall patted her on the leg and she leaned against him, obviously taking comfort in his nearness. It hurt my heart to see them together like that. I would never have that closeness with Khaemmalu and certainly not in front of other people.

Some time later, Panouk sent a message to confirm Ahmose had been taken to the House of Life and the priests would begin the embalming process immediately, all expenses of which would be paid by the Palace. I tried not to think about Ahmose laid out, naked, on a workbench while the priest sliced her open.

There were tears from each of us at some point during the day. Merytre and Sehener huddled in a corner to cry. Ettu and Half sat together on the couch. She consoled him when he suddenly burst into tears, and he did the same for her. Even Tall, standing in his usual spot to the side of the window, wiped away a few surreptitious tears.

I went to my bedchamber to cry in private. I didn't want any of the others to comfort me. It was Khaemmalu I wanted, but I felt far too weary to walk all the way down the stairs and out to the grounds, so I stayed in my bedchamber and cried alone.

How had everything suddenly gone so wrong? Ahmose was dead, Henuttawy had run away, taking with her any chance of me holding Pharaoh accountable for his deeds, and Tiye had been treating me like a fool ever since I arrived. At least Khaemmalu had forgiven me for not telling him about the babe. He might not trust me again just yet, but he wasn't angry anymore.

By morning, I couldn't bear to spend another moment in my chambers where I was surrounded by so much sadness. Visiting Tiye was out of the question, but I could break my fast with Henutmire. I hadn't seen her for several days, and if I left now before my maids arrived, I could avoid their lengthy morning attentions. Ettu frowned hard at my suggestion that I go out wearing the gown I had put on myself, but Sehener managed to stop crying long enough to make up my face and fix my wig.

Ettu escorted me to the dining chamber and I was glad it was her. She was the one most likely to keep her tears in check while we were out.

But when we got there, the air was heavy and everyone looked very solemn. I took my usual place near Henutmire. Her face was grave and she gave me a look that seemed loaded with significance. The serving women came to offer their platters and I made my selections. Only once they were gone did I lean towards Henutmire.

"Has something happened?" I asked quietly. "Everybody looks so sombre."

"You haven't heard?" she whispered back.

I shook my head.

"Hydna and Weren were caught," she said.

"Caught?" It took me a moment to realise what she meant, and when I did, my heart froze. "You mean…"

She nodded.

"I heard immediate action was taken," she said.

"What does that mean?"

She leaned closer so she could whisper even more softly.

"Execution. Surely you know, no man other than Pharaoh is permitted to touch an Ornament."

I could only blink at her. Of course, I knew the rules. Sutem was the one who first told me, the day he coaxed me down from Tiye's window and he refused to touch me while doing so. It was worth more than his job, he had said. Tiye also mentioned it when she told me about Hydna and Weren. Khaemmalu and I even discussed the ramifications if we were caught, but it had always been an abstract fear. Something to worry about, yes, but also something distant. Intangible. Now, suddenly, it was very, very real.

"They have already been…" My voice trailed away. I couldn't make myself say it.

"I heard their punishments were carried out at dawn," Henutmire said. "It is terrible, of course, but we all know the rules. Hydna should not have risked it, no matter how she felt about him. I wouldn't chance it myself. Not for anyone in the world."

I looked down at the bread in my hand, surprised to find I had shredded it to crumbs while she was talking. I knew the consequences, but they had never felt so real before. So certain. This was what I risked every time I snuck away into the shrubbery with Khaemmalu.

We said little after that and Henutmire left soon after. I stayed only long enough to finish my goat milk. I couldn't eat, not while I was still thinking about how a man and a woman had lost their lives this morning, and all because they had the misfortune to fall in love.

As we left the dining chamber, Ettu gave a heavy sigh.

"I assume you heard," she said.

"Henutmire told me." There was no need to clarify what she meant. Surely folk wouldn't be talking about anything else today.

"Such a terrible thing," she said.

I started to agree, but stopped when I noticed Panouk approaching. Anger burned in me, sudden and fierce. He was in charge of the Palace, and that meant he must have been involved in deciding Hydna and Weren's fate.

"Administrator," I said as he came into speaking distance. My tone was chilly and he gave me a somewhat surprised look.

"Lady Kassaya," he said. "Is everything all right?"

"I have just heard this morning's news," I said. "About Hydna and Weren."

His face changed, his mouth drooped, and I almost thought he looked unhappy.

"Yes," he said. "Most unfortunate. Pharaoh was very angry when he heard and insisted they be punished immediately."

"So it was Pharaoh's decision."

He gave me an enquiring look.

"But, of course," he said. "The penalty for such a thing is extremely severe. Pharaoh himself always makes the decision in the very rare instances where such an affiliation is uncovered." He gave me a careful look. "I am sure you realise it was not my decision."

I didn't want to lie to him. He had been unexpectedly good to me lately, and I felt bad about assuming such a drastic punishment was his decision.

Panouk came a little closer and lowered his voice.

"I assure you, Lady Kassaya," he said, "that in such cases, I do endeavour to ensure the parties are treated as sympathetically as possible."

He gave me a look that seemed loaded with significance, then nodded farewell and strode away. It was almost as if he hinted he had intervened. That perhaps Hydna and Weren didn't receive the harsh punishment designated for them. Did he, perhaps, let them run away together? I couldn't be sure, but his words, and the look he gave me, suggested there might be more to their fate than anyone realised.

CHAPTER 41

Back in my chambers, Ettu relayed the news to suitably horrified reactions from Merytre and Sehener. She also told them what Panouk said to me, although if she, like me, thought he hinted their fates mightn't be what everyone thought, she didn't say it.

Tall frowned as Ettu spoke and I remembered that when we first arrived, Amankhau had told me the men would be permitted to sleep in the stables, but then had them escorted immediately to the front gates. It was only later I learned that other than the guards who patrolled the grounds and who weren't permitted to enter the Palace itself, unmodified men weren't allowed within the gates.

I had never understood why Tall and Half were merely escorted out. Was it possible Panouk did what he could to spare folk from the harsh penalties of this place? I was seeing him in a new light since our recent conversations. Perhaps I had misjudged him.

The arrival of a runner interrupted Ettu's accounting of Hydna and Weren's misfortune. One look at the way he held himself told me this was most likely a summons from Pharaoh.

And indeed, the boy brought a request for me to dine with Pharaoh when he visited the Palace in two days' time.

Ettu was swift to accept for me. She had to, of course — I could hardly turn down such an invitation — but I did wish she would at least try to find an excuse for me.

"Don't even say it," I warned as soon as the door closed.

Merytre's face filled with pretended innocence, while Sehener looked genuinely confused. Ettu turned her back and I was sure it was so she could roll her eyes without anyone seeing.

"Don't say what?" Sehener asked.

"I think we must," Merytre said. "You will have to wear the gem he gifted you and he has already seen all your gowns that go with it."

"Oh, are we designing a new gown?" Sehener asked, instantly cheered.

"No," I said firmly. "No more new gowns."

I couldn't bear the thought of spending the next two days listening to their arguments with the sewers and being stuck with pins while they fitted me.

"But—" Merytre stopped when I shot her a fierce look.

"No. If I am to tolerate another meal with that man, it will be in a gown I already have. And I'm not wearing his wretched sapphire again."

"You must," Ettu said quickly. "You know that. I think we can work with the gowns you already have, as long as you wear his gem."

"Maybe we could take a couple apart and refashion them," Sehener suggested. "It would be less work than a new design, and we could manage it between the three of us."

"I notice nobody has asked for my help with all this reworking and sewing," Half said drily. "I suppose that indicates you think little of my needlework ability."

"Well, we have never seen you so much as hold a needle," Ettu said. "Although you are rather skilled with your woodcarving knife."

"I could cut the fabric for you," he said.

They smirked at each other as if exchanging a private joke the rest of us didn't understand.

"Shall we go look through my lady's gowns?" Sehener was already headed for the doorway. "I have some thoughts about which ones might work."

The other women followed her, leaving just me with just Tall, whose gaze followed Sehener until she was gone, and Half.

"That was well played, Princess," Half said. "It will do them good to have something other than their sorrow to focus on."

As if he thought the idea to refashion an old gown was my own.

Ettu, Merytre and Sehener passed the next two days busying themselves with a gown for me. There were still moments of sadness, and quite a few tears shed for Ahmose, but Half was correct that it helped for the women to be busy. They only made me try it on once, and I was relieved to discover this gown had far more fabric covering my breasts than the one designed for Min's festival.

As always, I had to endure a very lengthy preparation session from my maids prior to the dinner with Pharaoh. I passed the time trying to think of how I might make conversation with him without revealing my hatred and disgust.

I was still disheartened at the unravelling of my plan to expose him, although I also felt bad at being so upset about it. What kind of person was I to be thinking about the disruption to my own plans so soon after Ahmose's death?

"We have a surprise for you, my lady," Khensa said with a giggle as she straightened my wig. They had already changed it three times. I hoped the surprise wasn't that they were going to change it again.

"What is it?" I asked.

She produced a small bottle from her pouch.

"We got you some frankincense." Her voice was proud and I realised all the maids had stopped to watch my reaction. "Since you seemed to like it so much. I requested it for you myself."

"I went with her," Tuya added.

"Is it not a fine surprise?" Nebetah asked.

"Oh, yes." I stammered as I tried to find the right words. They must have thought I hinted I wanted frankincense when I asked if anyone was wearing it. "Very thoughtful of you."

They all beamed and Khensa very carefully applied the perfume to my throat and wrists. I tried not to smell it. It was the first time I had smelled frankincense since I spoke with Ishtar's spirit. Its absence was, perhaps, an indication she no longer lingered in the realm of the living.

"Did you have any trouble obtaining it?" I asked, feeling like I should say something else since they had gone to so much trouble.

"Not at all." Khensa's voice was breezy. "I only had to tell the butler you had a fondness for it and he handed it over."

I didn't ask which butler she meant. It surely wasn't Weren, and he was the only one I knew by name.

"Oh, your kohl is smudged a little," Ipu said. "Please hold still, my lady, and I will fix it."

"I can't see a smudge." Hemetre leaned closer, inspecting my face.

I obligingly held myself very still.

"Right there," Ipu said. "In the corner. It is just the tiniest bit, but it isn't perfect."

"Oh, I see it." Hemetre handed Ipu the little bottle of kohl. "It definitely needs fixing."

As they busied themselves with perfecting my appearance, I caught Abar's eye. She stared at me, a scornful look on her face. I was tempted to ask if she, too, had been involved in procuring the frankincense, although I knew she wouldn't have been. I held my tongue. It would be cruel to point out how disconnected she was from the rest of my maids.

"I suppose you have found out nothing else about my sister," she said, her tone as belligerent as ever.

"I am afraid not." There was no point telling her I had tried to find a way for her to see her sister's body. She would only accuse me again of talking and not doing.

Abar sneered. "I don't need your help anyway."

"We are all finished, my lady," Mutnofret said before I could reply. "You look beautiful."

"Stunning," Tuya added.

The others murmured their own compliments as they headed for the door. As always, Abar was the first one out, leaving me to ponder what she had meant.

I waited until after they left before I took the Eye of Horus amulet from my pouch.

"It doesn't go with your gown," Ettu said quickly. "And it will clash with the sapphire."

"I thought I could tie it around my wrist," I said. "Or even my ankle."

They could pin it to the underside of my skirts for all I cared, as long as there was a way for me to wear it. The amulet might be nothing more than a silly superstition, but today I needed the comfort of its promise.

Ettu didn't argue any further, only tied the amulet around my wrist. There was no way to hide it there, of course, and she frowned about that, but its weight against my skin soothed me. It was a promise of protection, real or not, and I might need every scrap of protection tonight.

To Sehener's delight, Ettu and Merytre decided she should be the one to accompany me to dinner with Pharaoh. She fairly skipped along the hallway as we left my chambers, although she quickly settled.

"I feel awful," she said to me. "I'm such a bad person for being excited about coming with you. I know the things he has done, but still—" she darted a look at me, gauging my reaction "— it is Pharaoh".

I supposed for someone who had grown up here, it must be thrilling to be in such close contact with their ruler. I wondered whether she realised he probably wouldn't even notice her, let alone acknowledge her. Maybe that didn't matter to Sehener, though. Most people would never come any closer to Pharaoh than seeing him from afar at a celebration, like the parade for Min. They didn't know how fortunate they were.

CHAPTER 42

$\mathcal{D}$inner was to be in the same chamber as Pharaoh always used when he visited the Palace of the Ornaments. As we turned down the final hallway and faced the row of guards, my legs were weak and my palms sweated. I resisted the urge to dry them on my gown.

He has forgotten his anger about the *senet* game, I told myself. He would have said something at the festival otherwise. He probably doesn't even remember it was me. The amulet around my wrist seemed to throb in time with my heartbeat. Safe, safe, safe, it promised.

I suffered the usual indignity of a guard running his hands over my body before they allowed me to enter. The serving woman brought me wine, but I had barely taken a sip of it before Pharaoh arrived.

He made his way to a bench and sat with a grunt. With a goblet in his hand, he gave me an expectant look, as if wondering why I wasn't already on my belly. Briefly, I considered refusing, but I couldn't. Once, when my plan was still a possibility, I might have entertained thoughts of making *him* grovel on his belly.

When I possessed a spell to make me so powerful I had no need to fear him.

But any chance of that died with Ahmose. Now, it seemed likely I would spend the rest of my life being expected to fawn over a man who had probably forgotten my name yet again while I tried to conceal my hatred of him.

I set down my wine and lay on my belly. He left me there for a long time. Longer than usual. At last, he grunted and I took that as permission to stand. He glanced towards the space beside him on the bench and I sat, resolving to make no attempt at conversation. Pharaoh wouldn't, so why should I?

The wait for dinner was interminable without conversation to pass the time. His hand wandered my thigh while I tried to pretend it wasn't. He grunted a couple of times and seemed perfectly content to just sit there, drinking his wine and squeezing my thigh. When dinner was ready, he rose and went to his table. Not that I expected him to invite me to go with him, or ask if I was ready to eat, but he didn't even so much as look at me.

I settled myself on my cushion and made my selections from the vast assortment the serving women presented. There was far too much for two people. Roasted pigeons. Stewed goat. Baked fish. Lentils mashed with garlic. Duck eggs. Root vegetables, figs, olives and sweet, crunchy onions. Watermelon and pomegranates. Three types of bread. I took a modest helping and focused my attention on my plate.

My mind whirled with thoughts I didn't want to have while I was with Pharaoh. Ishtar, Nebtu and Tabiry. Three women I knew of who had all undoubtedly met their fates at Pharaoh's hands. Hydna and Weren, and Pharaoh's decree that execution was required for two people who had the misfortune to fall in love against his rules. My now-defunct plan to expose his crimes. And Tiye's plan.

Her plan to replace Pharaoh might be all that stood between

his murderous impulses and safety for all the women who encountered him. Perhaps it didn't matter whether I knew what sort of man Pentaweret was. Tiye said he was a better man than Pharaoh. Maybe that was enough. Maybe it didn't even matter that the decision of who should be on the throne seemed far too big for any one person to make. The only thing that was important was stopping him, like my sister wanted.

"Have you received any messages from Ishtar?" I asked Pharaoh.

The words were out of my mouth before I realised what I was going to say. I wasn't even sure why I said it. Maybe I wanted to hear him pretend she was well. Maybe I hoped he would see in my face that I knew he lied. A chill washed over me, but it was already said.

I expected fury from him. Perhaps another overturned table. My leg muscles were already tensing, preparing for me to jump up and flee. The Eye of Horus amulet tied around my wrist was supposed to protect me. I almost laughed out loud at the thought. What was a mere wooden amulet compared to the fury of Pharaoh?

But Pharaoh did none of what I expected. Instead, he only looked at me.

"Who?" he asked.

I stared at him. Was he joking? He had mentioned her when we played *senet*. He asked if I knew she was more beautiful than me. He said my father should have sent her instead of me. He knew who she was then.

"My sister," I repeated.

You know her, I wanted to say. You killed her. You cannot have forgotten her already.

But Pharaoh only gave me a blank look and returned his attention to his food.

And I realised something. His favourites were his favourites only for so long as it pleased him. Once he was finished with them, he would forget them. Tiye might be Pharaoh's Favourite right now, but sooner or later, he would forget her too, and what then? She expected to be rewarded with a villa, but that wouldn't happen if Pharaoh tired of her. She would be just another forgotten woman, discarded once mighty Pharaoh decided she was no longer of any value to him. Just another faceless, nameless woman he no longer cared to remember.

Would he ever know Tiye was the one who plotted against him? When her plan came to fulfilment and Pharaoh was toppled from his throne, would there be a moment when he looked his once-favourite in the eyes and realised she was the instrument of his downfall?

As I stared at my food to avoid making eye contact with Pharaoh, the desire to see him stopped burned within me. However his downfall happened, I wanted to be there. I wanted to see it, and I wanted to be a part of it.

Tomorrow, I would tell Tiye I would help her put her son on the throne.

* * *

Kassaya's journey concludes in
Book Six: Hawk of the West

ALSO BY KYLIE QUILLINAN

Palace of the Ornaments Series

Book One: *Princess of Babylon*

Book Two: *Ornament of Pharaoh*

Book Three: *Child of the Alliance*

Book Four: *A Game of Senet*

Book Five: *Secrets of Pharaoh*

Book Six: *Hawk of the West*

The Amarna Age Series

Book One: *Queen of Egypt*

Book Two: *Son of the Hittites*

Book Three: *Eye of Horus*

Book Four: *Gates of Anubis*

Book Five: *Lady of the Two Lands*

Book Six: *Guardian of the Underworld*

The Amarna Princesses Series

Book One: *Outcast*

Book Two: *Catalyst*

Book Three: *Warrior*

See kyliequillinan.com for more books, including exclusive collections, and newsletter sign up.

ABOUT THE AUTHOR

Kylie writes about women who defy society's expectations. Her novels are for readers who like fantasy with a basis in history or mythology. Her interests include Dr Who, jellyfish and cocktails. She needs to get fit before the zombies come.

Swan – the epilogue to the Tales of Silver Downs series – is available exclusively to her newsletter subscribers. Sign up at kyliequillinan.com.